Book Two of the Real Dirty Duet

NEW YORK TIMES BESTSELLING AUTHOR

ABOUT REAL SEXY

In Nashville, country stars are a dime a dozen.
I swore I'd never get caught up with one, but Boone
Thrasher made a liar out of me.
I said I'd never put my heart on the line, but he didn't ask
before he stole it.
Now I'm facing my worst fears, and we'll see if this country
boy is tough enough to see it through.
Girls like me don't get happily-ever-afters . . . but maybe
he'll prove that wrong too.

Real Sexy is the conclusion to Boone and Ripley's story and
should be read after *Real Dirty*.

CHAPTER ONE

Twenty years earlier

"I ain't goin' nowhere with you." My father shouted the slurred words at the officer who walked into the Fishbowl only hours after Mama's body had been taken away.

I sat huddled in a corner, a pink wood-and-plastic guitar clutched in my arms. I didn't play it because Mama told me not to when Pop was around. It made him mad.

But he was already mad, and Mama was gone.

A few hours ago, I needed to pee. I wasn't supposed to be down in the bar while people were there unless Pop had me doing chores, but the bathroom upstairs wasn't working right. I tiptoed down the stairs, hoping he wouldn't catch me before I slipped into one of the stalls behind the door marked Cowgirls and Mermaids.

Except I never made it to one of the stalls. The dingy gray tile floor that I was in charge of mopping was stained dark red with a puddle around Mama.

"Mama?" I whispered, even though I knew she wouldn't answer. She was so quiet, so still.

A man lay facedown beside her in another dark puddle —the man who gave me the guitar—and he didn't move either.

I didn't know where the hysterical screaming was coming from until Pearl, one of the bar regulars I liked to pretend was my gran, burst into the bathroom, nearly plowing me over.

"Oh, sweet Jesus. Rip, get out of here. You shouldn't see this." She gagged before shoving me out the door.

But I'd already seen it, and I might have been only nine but I wasn't an idiot.

Mama was dead.

The man was dead.

And now the police thought Pop had something to do with it.

The bar cleared out as soon as word got around why there was a kid screaming in the bathroom, or maybe it was the way I'd run out yelling, "Mama's dead!" Either way, all the people pushed each other to get out of the bar, even as Pop hollered that they hadn't paid their tabs.

Now Pop's face was red as he argued with the policeman.

"You don't have a choice, Mr. Fischer. We're taking you in for questioning. Don't worry, your sister-in-law will stay with your daughter."

Like an afterthought, Pop glanced over at me in the corner, as if just remembering I existed. Aunt Laurelyn stood a dozen feet away with my cousin, Brandy, wrapped around her waist. She was only six, but she was as mean as any eleven-year-old I'd ever met. I didn't have any Barbies left because of her. She'd popped their heads off, or cut their hair and drawn on them with markers. When I complained to Mama, she'd told me I had to share because Brandy didn't have it as good as I did.

Her clothes were my worn-out hand-me-downs and her Keds were gray instead of the original white, so I guessed Mama was right. I still thought she was mean, though.

"Go on, Frank. I'll stay with the girls. I'll take them to McDonald's for a Happy Meal while the police . . . do what they need to do here." Aunt Laurelyn choked on the last few words.

"Don't care where you go, but make sure that bathroom gets cleaned up before I get back."

My stomach twisted at the thought of mopping up those puddles of blood.

"Nine isn't too young to learn what hard work is. It'll be good for her." That's what Pop told Mama when she said I shouldn't be cleaning the bar, only the apartment upstairs. Just like every other time, Pop won, and while I pushed the mop over pee and puke, I'd wondered why adults were so gross. Even grosser than kids.

I didn't dare complain, though, because Pop's temper scared me, especially when his words were slurring like they were now. That meant I'd end up getting smacked.

"Let's go, Mr. Fischer. The faster you leave, the faster we get this taken care of," the police officer with the freshly starched uniform said.

"Right, like I really believe that."

But instead of arguing more, Pop actually went with them. I didn't understand why they were taking him, but I guessed they had to have a reason or they wouldn't do it.

When the door closed behind them, leaving me, Aunt

Laurelyn, and Brandy alone, my aunt walked behind the bar, grabbed a bottle from the shelf, and poured herself a big glass. From the color, I assumed it was whiskey, because that's what Mama liked to drink.

Mama's dead.

My chest clenched and tears landed on my guitar.

Who could do that to her? Pop made her lip and nose bleed the week before last, but he couldn't . . . wouldn't . . . *Right?*

Aunt Laurelyn downed the glass of liquor before pouring some more. When she lifted it to her lips the second time, she paused.

"She shoulda known better." She whispered the words as tears welled in her eyes.

"What?"

Aunt Laurelyn drained the glass and lowered it to the bar.

"She shoulda known better than to get mixed up with Gil. I warned her." Aunt Laurelyn huffed out a harsh sound. "I knew messin' around with that man wasn't gonna get her anywhere good. And see what it got her?" Tears spilled down her cheeks.

For the first time since I came out of the bathroom screaming, Esteban, my mama's parrot, piped up.

"Dirty whore. Dirty whore."

Aunt Laurelyn sagged against the bar. "The whole world's gonna say worse, so I guess we better prepare for it. Let's get the hell out of here."

Two hours later, we came back from McDonald's and I stared at the bathroom door. The police were gone, and Mama was too.

Aunt Laurelyn took the bottle of whiskey and disappeared upstairs. I swallowed back the bile as I remembered what Pop had said about making sure the mess was cleaned up. Aunt Laurelyn sure wasn't gonna do it.

When I closed my eyes and saw Mama in that pool of blood, my Happy Meal twisted in my stomach, threatening to land on the floor.

They can't make me do it. I won't.

But when Pop came back a few hours later and found it wasn't done, he started yelling. Aunt Laurelyn didn't wake up, and Brandy hid.

My tears landed like raindrops as I dunked the mop in the water, turning it red.

Good-bye, Mama.

CHAPTER TWO

RIPLEY

Present day

Alone in Boone's empty house, I listen to Esteban squawk in his cage.

"Shoulda known better."

The bird has the most uncanny knack for saying the exact wrong thing at the wrong time.

"Shut up!"

"Crackerhead," he says before rustling his wings and preening.

When Anthony came out to the pond on his ATV to let Boone know the cops were here, he didn't say why. Boone hustled down the dock and they talked. From where I sat, I could hear Boone curse before coming back to get me.

All the questions were on the tip of my tongue to ask, but I held them back. I figured he would tell me when we got back to the house, but once we got there, everything was a whirlwind.

Boone strode to the front door and stepped outside with

Anthony on his heels. When they returned, it was for Boone to grab his wallet and press a hard kiss against my lips.

"Sit tight. I'll be back as soon as I can."

I couldn't hold my questions in any longer. "What the hell is going on, Boone? How could they have a warrant for your arrest? It doesn't make any sense."

"I'll take care of it. It's bullshit and an inconvenience, but it'll all be over soon."

That's when the thought struck me. "Oh shit. It's because of Esteban, isn't it? Did Brandy—"

"It'll be all right. Stay in the house, because guaranteed there are paps out front waiting to get a pic. Keep off that ankle."

Then he was gone, and I was left wondering if Boone is straight-up crazy.

Stay in the house. Don't worry about it. If that's what he really expects me to do, he's insane. He's been gone five minutes, and there's no way I'm going to sit here and wait.

This has to be because of Esteban, which means it's all my damn fault. If I didn't love that stupid parrot too much to let him starve under Pop and Brandy's care, none of this would have happened.

He's basically mine in every way that matters. You know, except *legally*.

Esteban belonged to Mama, and now Pop, but the only reason he's still alive to talk shit to me is because I've taken care of him for the last twenty years. Pop hasn't done anything but swear at him for as long as I can remember.

And I dragged Boone into this mess because I just *had* to rescue the bird.

Shit.

Is there anything I can't screw up? I shouldn't have asked

for his help. I should have asked Hope for her truck and handled it myself.

I hobble over to my purse and pick up the phone to call my best friend. Hope has tonight off, and we were supposed to go out to dinner if I was back from Boone's in time.

I hate that I've only called her when I need a favor lately, but she knows I'd do anything for her, so that lessens the guilt somewhat.

She answers on the second ring, a smile in her voice. "Hey, girl. What's happening? I keep seeing pictures of you and that sexy country boy online. I swear, the photographers are having a field day trying to outdo each other. You look so freaking cute together, though."

"Do you think you could come get me?"

A moment of silence hangs on the line before she replies. "Oh shit, did it already go south? I'm so sorry, honey. What did that jackass do?"

I laugh at the quick change in her attitude. That's what you call a true friend.

"Not in the way you think, but I need a ride, and my car is at your place."

"Of course. What's the address?"

I walk over to the counter where there are a few pieces of mail waiting to be dealt with, and pick one up to rattle off the address.

"I have no clue where that is, but I'll google. I'll be there as soon as I can. But tell Boone I'm going to castrate him if he hurt you."

We hang up before I tell her he's not here.

Forty-five minutes later, I head to the end of the driveway as I see headlights pull up to the gate. I'm in my jeans from the night before, and a stolen T-shirt of Boone's tied in a knot at the bottom to keep it from hanging down to my knees.

From my quick scan of the area, I don't see any sign of cars other than Hope's big truck, but that doesn't mean the paps aren't hiding somewhere. Boone taught me that.

"How do I open this gate?" I mumble. I know Boone has a sensor in his car, but there's no obvious mechanism for opening it from the inside. *Am I going to have to climb it?*

I can just imagine the tabloid pictures and headline.

BOONE THRASHER'S GIRLFRIEND SO DESPERATE TO GET AWAY, SHE CLIMBS GATE IN STOLEN SHIRT

But nothing I do will make the thing budge. Out of options, I grab the metal bar and haul myself up.

Hope pops out of the truck as I throw a leg over the top. My ankle is throbbing, but thankfully the pain is bearable.

"What the hell are you doing?" Hope hurries over to the gate and bear-hugs my legs so I can slide down her body.

Please let there be a merciful God and no pictures of this. Otherwise, the headlines are now going to read:

BOONE THRASHER'S GIRLFRIEND ESCAPES COMPOUND INTO THE ARMS OF HER LESBIAN LOVER

"I didn't have a choice. I had to get out, and I don't know how to work the damn thing. Do you?"

She shakes her head. "No. But let's get the hell out of here before someone thinks we're trying to break in and not out."

Crap, I hadn't even thought about that. I round the hood to the passenger side of the truck and climb inside.

"How's the ankle?" Hope asks as I shut the door.

"Still aches, but I'll be fine. I've had worse sprains and kept working. Boone overreacted." To myself I add, *And maybe I'm downplaying it a tiny bit.*

Hope shifts the truck into reverse and backs out of the driveway. "Maybe so, but it was still super hot to see him go all alpha-protective mode and carry you out of the White Horse. Have you seen the pictures? I think everyone with a cell phone managed to snap a different angle. Some people are calling him the Gentleman Bad Boy now."

I roll my eyes. "What else did I miss?"

"One site said you fainted because you're pregnant with his love child." Hope glances at my giant shirt. "If they see you in that, they'll be on baby-bump watch."

This time when I roll my eyes, my vision blurs for a second, and I'm a little concerned I might strain an eye muscle. If that's even possible. "Good God."

"I mean, you did go to the hospital right after, and they didn't miss that information." When I release a low groan, Hope continues. "Did you really think dating him would be easy?"

It's on the tip of my tongue to say that we're not dating,

but I hold back the protest because actually, I have no idea what we're doing now.

Before today, I would have said it's nothing but a rebound fling for Boone, but things have . . . shifted. I don't have an answer for her, so I say nothing.

Hope takes a left and heads for the highway, keeping the conversation going without waiting for me to reply. "So, you want to tell me what's going on that necessitates a midnight escape plan?"

"It's not midnight, and I'm not escaping."

Hope glances over at me. "You scaled a fence."

"I told you I don't know how to open it. Boone and Anthony had to leave in a hurry." I hesitate for only a second before I fill her in on the arrest.

"Holy fucking shit. That's going to take all of five seconds to hit the news cycle. But what the hell could he be arrested for?"

"It has to be my fault. I swear to God, if Brandy is behind this, I'm going to rip the hair out of her head like she used to do to my Barbies."

Hope knows all about my long-standing issues with Brandy. "You really think she'd do that?"

"There's not much I'd put past her at this point."

When Hope merges onto the highway, she glances at me. "Then we best go find out from the source, don't you think?"

CHAPTER THREE

RIPLEY

The OPEN sign flickers in the high window next to the fluorescent fishbowl. The fish blinks as though his light is about to burn out. Except for the few cars belonging to regulars, there are hardly any vehicles parked out front.

"Place is hoppin', isn't it?" Hope says, sarcasm rich in her tone as we pull around the block to park in the back.

"Like always."

Brandy doesn't have a car, but I have to believe if the bar is open, then she's gotta be here and working. It's somewhat shocking to think of her getting to work on time and managing to open the place.

Then again, now that I'm not here to stop her from skimming unlimited money from the till, she has a better incentive.

I shove down the bittersweet pang as I carefully make my way to the back door, my ankle twinging from my climb over the fence. When I push open the door, Earl, Pearl, and Jim are in their customary places at the bar. A quick scan reveals a half dozen unfamiliar faces nursing drinks, and a few pairs of eyes light up when they catch sight of me.

Gossip seekers?

It seems about right. Or maybe they're thinking that if I show, maybe Boone will come too.

Glad they don't know the reason that won't be happening.

"What the hell are you doing here?" Brandy's voice snaps out from behind the bar like a bullwhip. "You aren't welcome and you know it, so just turn around and crawl back to wherever you came from."

Brandy's face is caked with thick makeup, especially around her cheekbone. Her contouring looks like shit. On a regular day, it's her eye makeup that looks the worst—heavy eyeliner with even heavier smudging.

I close the distance to the bar and stop at the end. "What did you do?"

Earl, Pearl, and Jim all hunch forward as though making sure they don't miss a single word of this.

Brandy's hand shakes, and she splashes liquor on the wood instead of making it all inside the shot glass. "I don't know what you're talking about."

"Bullshit."

I lean in closer and pitch my words low, hoping my audience doesn't hear them. "You called the cops." Brandy's gaze darts away. "Is this about Esteban? You hate that bird, so this is ridiculous."

"I'm not talking to you," she says, her voice low and harsh.

"Because you're full of shit. I swear to you that I'm going to make you regret whatever lies you've told the cops. You understand me? They don't take kindly to people wasting their time."

She slams the liquor bottle down on the counter. "That damn bird wasn't yours to take. Uncle Frank was pissed."

That I have a hard time believing. "He's wanted to get rid of Esteban for years. No way Pop would go through all this trouble to get him back."

Brandy's gaze shifts away again and my gut tells me I'm missing something, but she's not going to tell me a thing.

"Fine. I'll leave, but you better believe I'm gonna figure out exactly what you did, and you're going to regret it."

"More like you're gonna regret getting mixed up with Boone Thrasher. I always knew you were going to be just like your mama. Too bad the bird's not here to call it like it is, but my mom and I see it plain as day."

I know what she's talking about—Esteban squawking one of his favorite phrases—*dirty whore*. Then the word *mom* slams into me.

"Wait, what does Aunt Laurelyn have to do with anything? Is she here?"

"Not yet, but she'll be here soon. We're gonna turn this bar around and make bank. It'll be just like it always should've been now that you're out of the way."

Laurelyn stepped in and ran the bar during those first few weeks after Mama died, and Pop barely crawled out of bed except to get another bottle. Once he pulled himself together, he told her to get the hell out, that he couldn't stand to see her face anymore because she looked too much like Mama. Aunt Laurelyn took Brandy and moved to Memphis the next day. I used to wish she'd taken me too, and part of me resented her for leaving me with Pop. I haven't seen her in ages.

"I've been trying to dig this place out of a hole for years, and if I couldn't, there's no way you'll be able to."

Brandy flips her hair, drawing my eyes once again to her shitty makeup job. "We both know my mama was always better at serving drinks than fucking the customers, *unlike yours*."

"Shut your damn mouth, Brandy."

"Not till you get out of *my bar!*"

Hope steps up beside me, and I can feel the rage rolling off her in waves. If we don't leave now, she might be the one to take out Brandy, and I'm not about to risk my cousin calling the police again.

"Fine. I'll go. But first, you have to tell me how you paid the fire marshal fines already and managed to get all those safety upgrades in place."

Brandy's lips twist into a mocking smile. "I didn't."

I shake my head. "You're an idiot. He'll be back, and he'll shut this place down."

With a smug look, Brandy picks at her nails. "Good thing it's none of your business anymore."

The thought of the Fishbowl being closed for good tugs at my heart, but there's nothing I can do now. I need to let it go. *But how?*

"Good luck. You're going to need it." I turn to Hope. "Let's go."

As I follow her out of the bar, a feeling of finality settles in my bones and tears sting my eyes.

I'm sorry I couldn't do better, Mama.

I pause in the doorway and take one last look behind me. I memorize the smell, the feel, the pictures of the stars on the walls, and tuck it all deep inside me.

The best and worst moments of my life happened here, and I'm no longer welcome. The thought burns, and I suck in a breath and bite my lip.

I'm not saying good-bye, Mama, because you're not here anymore. It's just a building.

When I step outside, the sense of loss threatens to overwhelm me.

Once we're in the truck, Hope fires up the engine. "You going to be okay?"

"I don't really have a choice, do I?"

Instead of putting the truck in gear, Hope looks over at me. "For what it's worth, I think you made the right decision. Your mom would want more for you than to be trapped in that bar under your dad's thumb. It's time for you to figure out what *you* want, Ripley. The world's a lot bigger than those four walls."

"I know." And I do. Hope is speaking the truth, but I haven't exactly had time to cope with the huge changes in my life, let alone a chance to figure out what I want.

Hope pulls out of the parking lot and points the truck in the direction of her apartment. "What now?"

"Maybe—" My phone vibrates, interrupting me. Law's name pops up on the screen.

Why would he be calling?

"You gonna answer that?"

I look at Hope as I pick up the call. "Hello?"

"You still with that guy? The one from last night?" Law's voice is hurried and tense.

"What are you talking about?"

"The country singer. Boone Thrasher. Are you really with him?"

"What does it matter, Law?" It's on the tip of my tongue to tell him there's no chance we're ever getting back together, but he keeps talking.

"I got called into work to do some research for a partner

tonight. A criminal law partner that represents Boone Thrasher."

Dread curls in my belly. "What kind of research?"

"Assault and battery. That's what he got arrested for. You really want to date a woman beater, Rip?"

CHAPTER FOUR

BOONE

It's been a long time since I had my ass shoved in a cell. Back then, I paced the floor, pissed off that I was stupid enough to get caught drinking with my buddies in a building set for demolition the next day, but glad that they'd gotten away, even if I hadn't.

My dad didn't speak for most of the ride after he bailed me out a few hours later, but when we got home, he parked the truck in the drive and turned to me.

"I'm thinking you already know you don't want to be spending any more nights in jail."

Somehow his quiet question made the shame more acute than a tirade would have. "No, sir."

"Then use your head, Boone. The Lord has bigger plans for you than this, so don't prove him wrong."

"Yes, sir."

"Apologize to your mama when you get inside. She's been worried sick about you."

"Yes, sir." Guilt flooded me next.

After I tromped into the house and apologized to Ma,

that was the end of it. My parents never spoke of it again. Never took me to task. Somehow, they knew that the ass-ripping I was giving myself was worse than any they could deliver. They were right, as my folks usually are.

As I lean up against the cool concrete wall of this cell, my hat pulled down low, all I can think about is how deep this is gonna cut Ma when she hears it. She'll know it's not true because I'd never hit a woman, but some people in our small town won't be so kind about it.

She's been a target more than once because of my antics, and that's part of the reason I've tried to clean up my act.

I can imagine those catty women whispering about it behind her back. She'll say she doesn't care, but I still hate that I put her in this position, especially over something I clearly didn't do.

This is so insane, I'm still reeling from the charges.

It isn't the first time someone has accused me of some-thing, thinking I would be an easy target more likely to pay them off than create a big stink that could affect my reputa-tion, but those people don't know me.

I've shown up at more than one person's house or apart-ment, asking them to explain how some of the stuff they've accused me of could have happened. I always make sure it's recorded too, just so I have something to show the cops. Turns out that a lot of people who think they're going to get rich quick off me don't have the balls to lie to my face. I'm hoping like hell this is going to be the same kind of situation.

The media is going to crucify me if I can't get Brandy to drop the charges and issue a public statement pretty fucking quick. Even then, it might already be too late. Regardless, I'll be vindicated. I'd never put my hands on a woman in anger, and that lying bitch knows it's true.

I don't care that she's Ripley's cousin; she's going down for filing a false police report at the very least. I have a hard time believing Ripley will argue with that, because from what I've seen, Brandy sure doesn't treat her like any kind of family I've ever had.

And fuck, *Ripley*. She's stuck at my place, not sure what the hell is going on. I feel like shit that I couldn't take the time to explain, but I wasn't about to drag her outside with the cops and let some asshole with a long lens get a picture of her caught up in this mess. Those frigging paparazzi are like some unholy combination of cockroach and vulture lately. Scuttling out of nowhere and picking at the bones until there's nothing left.

Like I told Ripley, my privacy is what I miss the most, and I miss it even more now that she's in my life.

If she's in my life much longer.

No, there's no way she'll believe Brandy's accusation.

But it's Brandy's word against mine, and she's the one with the wicked shiner, according to the pictures the cops shoved in my face.

They didn't care that I said I didn't touch her, just told me to tell it to the judge. They were the second type of cop you run into in Nashville. Type one being the kind who will usually let things slide if you're a celebrity. Type two is the hard-ass who wants to make sure you're not getting any special treatment at all due to your status. I don't usually care either way, but this time, it's bullshit.

"Thrasher, you're sprung," a guard's voice calls out as he walks down the hall to slide the cell door open.

Thank fuck.

I don't know what strings my agent and my lawyer had to pull, and I don't care how much it cost me, but I'm glad to be walking out of here.

At least I am until I hit the lobby and see the cameras flashing in the direction of the woman waiting for me. As I step through the door, she runs and throws herself into my arms.

"I came as fast as I could, baby. Everything's going to be just fine now."

I'm stunned and motionless as Amber plants her lips on mine.

CHAPTER
FIVE

N o. Way. In. Hell.

That's what I told Law when he said that Boone has been charged with assault and battery *by my own damned cousin.*

When I whispered, "I'm going to kill her," Law stopped me and said I better not say things like that because he'd be ethically bound to report it if he thought I was serious.

I hung up on him.

"What the fuck is going on?" Hope asks as she pulls into a parking space near her building.

"I don't know, but it sounds like a whole lot of crap to me."

I fill her in on everything Law just told me. I'm of half a mind to go right back to the Fishbowl and confront Brandy, but after her outright lying to the cops and then lying to me only fifteen minutes ago, I know it's not going to do me any good. Worst-case scenario, I end up in jail too because I actually beat the crap out of her.

I know, in my heart of hearts, that Boone didn't touch her.

And I have a way to prove it.

"I need my laptop."

"Why?"

"I hooked up a DIY security-camera system in the bar a while ago because I wanted to figure out who was skimming from the till. I'm hoping the camera angles are going to be able to prove that Boone didn't touch Brandy."

"That's freaking brilliant."

I shrug. "It would've been even more brilliant if I'd updated my phone to download the app so I could watch the feed anywhere, but I never bothered after I saw it was obviously Brandy."

Hope turns to me, an eyebrow raised. "Why didn't you fire her ass or tell your dad?"

"I knew it wouldn't matter. For some reason, she can do no wrong in his eyes."

"While you can do no right," she finishes for me.

It's the sad truth, so I reach for the door handle instead of responding.

As soon as we're in the apartment, I pull my laptop out of my stuff in the living room and log on to the website where my camera feeds run. They only back up for a few days at a time because I didn't have the cash to spring for a bajillion bytes of extra storage, but we were only there yesterday, so I should be able to see everything.

I type the approximate time we got to the Fishbowl into the search bar and wait for the video to populate.

After I skip forward a little bit, the video shows the door swinging open and Boone walking inside. Hope leans over my shoulder to watch.

"I know this isn't the appropriate time or place for this observation, but he is one fine-as-hell man."

It's on the tip of my tongue to say *and you haven't even seen him naked*, when I realize I haven't seen him fully naked either. *Not important, Ripley. First, you get his ass out of the jail cell your lying bitch of a cousin put him in, and then you get to see that ass naked.*

We both watch as the recording plays on the screen without sound. It's clear that Boone and Brandy have words, and I wish we could hear them.

"He looks pissed," Hope whispers, the concern in her voice coming through loud and clear.

"He would never hit her." To myself, I add, *Unless I've completely and totally misjudged him.*

No. I don't believe that. Not for a second.

"If you say so, I trust you."

But she doesn't have to take my word for it because we watch the rest of the recording, and it ends with Boone walking out of the bar without laying a finger on her. Hell, he even gave her money, which means we could argue that he bought and paid for Esteban. *Not that she deserves another dime.*

"That lying skank!" Hope shoots up from her crouch behind me and paces. "What are we going to do?"

I glance at my friend, with her hands balled into fists like she'd like to beat the crap out of Brandy herself. "I need to tell Anthony. They have to get the recording to the police."

"Who is Anthony again?"

"Boone's head of security."

"Okay. Makes sense. Then what?"

"Then Boone gets out of jail, and I figure out what I'm going to do about Brandy."

"She should be the one arrested."

I'm not about to disagree with Hope on that one.

It's a long, sleepless night, because even though I tried to contact Anthony, his phone went straight to voice mail and he never returned my messages. Same with Boone's, although that doesn't surprise me. *It's not like they let you have cell phones in lockup.*

I toss and turn on the futon, wondering if the fancy partner Law works for has managed to get Boone out yet, or whether he's going to be in there all night. He hasn't called me, so I'm assuming that means nothing good has happened.

Unless he decided he's done with me because my crazy-ass cousin got him arrested.

The shaft of pain that stabs through me at that thought almost takes my breath away. He wouldn't just never contact me again, right? No. Of course not. I tell myself to settle down, but one thing can't be denied.

I'm not ready to be done with him.

That fact alone scares me because I've gotten more attached to Boone than I realized. He and I live in two different worlds, and just because we found some common ground doesn't mean that it's going anywhere.

Except . . . isn't that what he said he wanted? To see where this goes?

When sunlight streams through the cracks in the drapes, the sounds of Hope waking up filter through the small apartment. I hear her curse in the kitchen before she shuffles into the living room, a hand covering her mouth as she yawns.

"I totally forgot to get more coffee yesterday, so we're out. I'm gonna run down to the shop on the corner. You want some?"

After the sleepless night I had, I need an IV drip of caffeine. "That sounds amazing."

"Caramel latte with an extra shot sound good?"

"Heavenly."

"I'll be right back. You can take the first shower while I'm gone, if you want."

"Thank you for being so awesome." I reach out and grab Hope's hand.

"That's what friends are for." She squeezes my fingers and presses a kiss to my head.

After Hope shoves her feet into shoes and slips out of the apartment, I roll off the futon and check my phone for the fiftieth time, even though it hasn't made a sound.

I head for the bathroom with it clutched in my hand. I have to get in touch with Anthony ASAP. If Boone is still in jail . . . It makes me sick to think about it. If I don't hear from Anthony within the hour, I'll go straight to the police myself to get Boone out.

Decision made, I let the stream of water soak my hair as my mind drifts to Brandy and how she looked last night. I knew there was something screwed up about her caked-on makeup. It's not the first time I've seen Brandy use a load of concealer around her eye and cheekbone, but when I asked in the past, I'd get a lethal stare in return. I always assumed some shitty guy she hooked up with had smacked her around, and I couldn't help but pity her. She knew she always had a place to stay with me, but she didn't use it.

I think that's why I waited so long to confront her about skimming from the till. Even though she's a pain in my ass and can make my life hell, I've always felt bad for Brandy. Her dad was never in the picture, and from the little she told me about how things were in Memphis, my aunt wasn't exactly mother of the year.

Brandy showed up back in Nashville when she was eighteen, saying she needed a place to stay because Aunt Laurelyn kicked her out and told her it was time to make her own way. What could we do but try to help her? She had no support other than Pop and me. She'd work at the bar for a few months until she lost interest, and then she would stop showing up and move in with some boyfriend and do something different for a while. Every damn time, she came back, and Pop always made me give her a job. When we knew he wasn't moving back upstairs after his accident, he told me to let Brandy have the spare room. So I did. Whenever Brandy's life went sideways, I came to the rescue.

And this is how she repays me.

It shouldn't be such a shock. I was the only one expected to put family loyalty at the top of my priority list. But Brandy finally crossed a line that can't be uncrossed, and I'm *done*.

I hurry through the rest of my shower, not wanting to use all the hot water, and I hear the door shut as Hope returns.

"Rip?"

"I'm almost done." I shut off the water and grab the towel I tossed over the curtain rod.

"You're gonna want to see this."

Her wary tone alerts me to the fact that something is

definitely wrong. With water still beaded on my skin and dripping from my hair, I wrap the towel around myself and open the bathroom door.

"What's going on?"

She holds out her phone. The red banner across the top of the screen is the name of a gossip site that wants to be the next TMZ.

I squint and step closer to read the headline of an article posted only a half hour ago.

BOONE THRASHER AND AMBER FLEET REUNITED

Beneath it is a picture of Amber wrapped around Boone like a spider monkey as she kisses him.

"What the fuck?" I whisper.

CHAPTER SIX

BOONE

An hour earlier

The door to the Escalade slams shut before the vehicle pulls away with Amber and me inside.

Eyeing her like she's a viper poised to strike, I try to figure out what angle she's working. "What the hell are you doing here?"

Amber shifts in her seat to face me, and it stuns the crap out of me that I was planning to ask her to marry me nine days ago. *What a dumbass.* Now when I look at her, everything comes off as manufactured, from her rhinoplastied nose to her collagen-injected lips.

"Saving your ass. What does it look like?"

"It looks like you're trying to stage some kind of goddamned reconciliation, and you know that shit isn't happening."

She rolls her eyes. "You could be a little more grateful. I just dropped a pile of cash to bail you out of jail."

"You'll get your money back within the hour. Where the

fuck did you come from, and where the hell is your husband?" I emphasize the word *husband*, hoping she realizes just how frigging ridiculous it is that she showed up here.

"I don't have a husband. The marriage has already been dissolved. It was just a big misunderstanding."

Remnants of the anger I felt when I first found out what Amber had done flare up. "A misunderstanding? You call getting married a fucking misunderstanding?"

She waves a hand. "You know I stayed in Vegas the day after my show for a meeting. Well, that meeting was with a big-shot Hollywood producer to talk about my acting career . . . and things got a little crazy."

"Crazy? Yeah, that's exactly what it was when I heard that my goddamned girlfriend was married." My temper kicks up another notch.

"He made promises, Boone! He swore he was going to get me a starring role in the next Ryan Gosling movie he's producing, and that's where things get fuzzy."

"I can't fucking wait to hear this."

To her credit, Amber's cheeks turn pink.

"We went out, had some drinks, did some blow and some pills, and the next thing I know, we're at a wedding chapel and he told me it was my big audition. All I had to do was walk down the aisle and I'd be Hollywood's next big thing. So I did. Then I woke up the next morning with a ring on my finger, lying next to a guy I only vaguely remember—one I never would've touched without being seriously fucked up. I mean, God, you should've seen his receding hairline and tiny dick. The first thing I told him was I wanted the contract for my movie role, and that's when he told me it was already taken and I'd have to build up to something that big. He lied to me!"

And what bothers her the most about this situation is that he lied to her . . . If I'd been carrying a single shred of regret for not trying to patch things up with Amber, it would have died right then. Luckily for me, I've already moved way the fuck on. Hell, I dodged a bullet.

"I would say you've gotta be joking, but that's too sad not to be true. Sorry 'bout your luck and your big splashy Hollywood career that ain't happenin'. Now, tell me what was the point of coming here and making a big scene? Anything between us is dead. Done. Over."

The flush of embarrassment fades from her cheeks as her eyes take on a calculating gleam. She stretches an arm out and lays her hand on my thigh.

"Oh, Boone, we're not even close to over. I need you now more than ever."

The SUV drives away, leaving me at the corner near my agent's building. No way was I going to let the press follow Amber's SUV all the way to my place, and that's on top of the fact that I don't want to spend thirty minutes letting her explain why she thinks what she did was no big deal, and how we can "save each other" by getting back together.

Call me old fashioned and a little bit country, but it's a big fucking deal. I wouldn't tie myself to Amber again if my balls were on fire and she was the only person who could put them out.

I scan the street, hoping the press isn't on me already,

and duck into the building. The security guard at the desk stands up when I walk in.

"Sir—" he starts.

I tip up the bill of my hat, and his eyes widen in recognition.

Yeah, man. I'm not the one you're trying to keep out.

There was a time years ago when he might have thrown me out for trying to get a meeting with an agent, but those days are over.

I ride the elevator up to Nick's office, hoping like hell he's actually here. When the receptionist catches sight of me, she straightens in her seat.

"Mr. Thrasher, did you have an appointment? I don't recall—"

I ignore her and push right through the door that leads into the inner sanctum, Nick's slick corner office. She reaches for the phone, but I'm going to beat her there.

"Where the fuck were you?" I don't bother with a greeting as I shove open his door.

Inside, a young, skinny blonde, who looks like she's more likely to be another wannabe Britney Spears than a country girl, sits perched on the edge of the expensive leather chair. But then again, couldn't someone say that about Amber? That she would fit in better climbing the pop charts in LA than she does in Nashville's country scene?

Nick sighs. "I'm sorry, Jerrica, we'll have to continue this later."

She rises to her pink pumps with a smile aimed in my direction.

Another Barbie lookalike. Perfect. Just what this town needs.

Once she's out of the office, I stride to the window and look out over the city I love. Music City. Where I belong.

When I spin around, I toss another question at Nick since he hasn't answered my first. "Where were you? Did you know she was coming?"

Nick lowers himself back into his fancy leather chair after letting the blonde out and crosses his arms. "I'd be a little more concerned about the charges than your girl-friend picking you up."

"Ex-girlfriend," I growl through gritted teeth.

"Ex-girlfriend," he says, correcting himself. "But you know, it's worth pointing out that if you were still with Amber and had never gotten mixed up with this Ripley girl, none of this would have happened. I told you to stay away from her. Keep a low profile. But you didn't listen. You gonna listen now? Because putting some distance between you two would be the best thing for you."

"Are you shitting me? You want to put this all on Ripley?"

"Her cousin got you thrown in jail."

"Because she's a bitch with an ax to grind. I didn't touch her!"

"I believe you, Boone. Trust me, I do. But . . . right now, Charity is fielding calls from dozens of people wanting details. You're a role model for a lot of kids, and when word travels about this, your reputation is going to take a huge hit. The best thing is to find something to divert the atten-tion while we sort this out." He pauses before leaning forward on his desk. "Have you considered the possibility of reconciling with Amber? People loved seeing you together. It was a fairy tale they could get behind."

I can't believe the words coming out of his mouth.

"Are you fucking kidding me? Instead of the press thinking I'm a woman beater, you want them to think I'm a doormat who lets his girlfriend marry and fuck another guy before taking her back?"

"Look, I know it sounds bad, but—"

"No. Not fucking happening, and if you suggest it again, we're done. Now I gotta get my financial manager on the phone and make sure he wires Amber's account with whatever she laid out for my bond. Unless you've got something useful to say, I'm gonna go wait in another office for my ride."

CHAPTER SEVEN

I've trolled way more gossip sites in the last hour and a half than I'll ever admit, torturing myself by reading articles about Amber and Boone being back together.

Of course this would happen to me. I should have known better.

Why did I think I was special? I'm such an idiot. He didn't even need my help getting out of jail.

Yeah, so positive self-talk isn't exactly my strong suit, but when you're constantly getting smacked down by life, it makes you realize that some things are better left alone. I should have known that having any kind of relationship with someone like Boone was a joke from the beginning.

Why did I even let myself start to think . . .

Hope comes out of the bathroom, leaving a cloud of hair spray behind her. "Babe, I gotta get to the bar for a meeting and to train a couple new people. Are you sure you want to come in tonight? Is your ankle really feeling okay?"

I look up at her from my sprawled position on the futon

where I've been throwing my pity party, and toss my phone on the coffee table.

One good thing in my life? I have an awesome friend.

"You know I love you, right?"

She tilts her head to the left, but her hair doesn't move, courtesy of the hair spray. Which makes me think of Pearl and her Aquanet with a stab of nostalgia.

"Are you drunk? Because you can't come to work if you're already—"

"No, I'm not drunk. I'm just telling you how much I appreciate you, and how lucky I am to have you. Thank you for everything you've done. Even when I'm swirling down the drain in an avalanche of shit, you're right there throwing me a lifeline."

Hope crosses the room and leans down to hug me. "You weren't swirling the drain, girl. You were staging a prison break." She stands straight again and looks me in the eye. "You've been trapped for so damn long that you don't have any idea what it's like to be free to think about doing anything but working like a slave at the Fishbowl. Maybe you should take some time away from the tabloid shit and think about what *you* want. You could go to school, get a certificate of some kind, or just get a different job."

Hope's words kick-start my brain in a way that's almost too overwhelming. Working at the Fishbowl, and now the White Horse, is all I've ever known, and thinking about anything else is a hair away from terrifying.

My best friend must read my fear all over my face. "Look, you don't have to decide right now. The job at the White Horse is yours for as long as you need it, but I really think you should take this chance to figure out what you really want to do."

"I'll think about it." I force a smile to my lips. "But, seriously, you said it—working behind a bar is all I know. I understand the rhythm and the flow. It's easy and feels like home to me. Anything else . . . is really hard to imagine."

"Take a couple hours. You don't have to be in until six. Open-mic night starts at eight, so you might want to bring your earplugs because some of those poor bastards are terrible." She glances up at the ceiling. "But thank God for Auto-Tune . . . because that means record labels don't need artists to have a decent voice if they're marketable. Anyhow, you good driving your car tonight too?"

My Javelin has been parked on the street near Hope's place since the day I quit the Fishbowl.

"Yep. No problem. I can drive. Thank you for everything, Hope."

"Love you, girl."

"Love you more."

As soon as the door shuts behind her, I lift my feet onto the futon and wrap my arms around my knees.

What do I want to do? Hell, what do I *like* to do? Who do I want to *be*? It's sad I don't have answers to any of those questions.

In a rare moment of solitude, I let my mind wander. It goes straight to Boone, and I want to kick my own ass.

I know tabloid pictures can skew the facts of what really happened, and there's a good chance that Boone didn't do a damn thing wrong, but it still cuts deep to see Amber Fleet wrapped around him like she has every right to be there.

Why am I even surprised?

The moment one thing starts going right in my life, *of course* it's bound to go down in flames in a morbidly spectacular fashion.

Ripley Fischer doesn't get to have the fairy tale. I'm just a homeless girl with a dead mom, a lying bitch of a cousin, and a dad who'd just as soon slap me around as crack open a beer. My life is never going to be one of those inspiring stories. It's just the same as it has always been—one step above shit.

I don't know why I thought this thing with Boone would be any different.

It's over. Now the only thing left to do is to clean up the mess that dragging my shit into his life caused.

But even if it's over, I have to clear Boone of the charges Brandy brought. Maybe he didn't need my help getting out of jail, but that doesn't mean the security feed isn't going to help him get free of this crap. Then I can walk away with a clean conscience and forget this whole thing ever happened. *Or just remember it late at night while I'm wishing my life was different.*

First things first. I need to spend more time going over the feed from the morning Boone and I went to the bar to see if there's anything else that could possibly help get Brandy's trumped-up charges thrown out. If Anthony doesn't get back to me, I have to take it to the police for evidence and hope they take me seriously. More than anything, I'm worried it'll get lost in the process and the right people won't see it, and Boone won't be exonerated.

Or you could put your big-girl panties on and just give it to Boone so he can get it to the right people. I know exactly what I'm trying to do. Avoiding facing him, knowing that he and Amber are back together and I have no right to touch him.

The thought burns, and I swallow back the lump in my throat before straightening my shoulders. That's exactly what I need to do. Maybe it'll kill any feelings I have for him, and I can move on with my life.

I can do this. Who cares if it's going to be awkward as shit, especially if Amber Fleet is still trying to surgically attach herself to him.

I hate the jealousy that eats through my veins like acid.

He's not mine. I have no claim on him and I never will, so *stop it.* Focus on things that matter. Like *who hit Brandy?*

My best guess is that she really was hiding a bruise under that makeup, because I have a hard time believing the cops would have hauled someone like Boone off to jail like that without serious proof.

I flip open the laptop and decide that while I'm considering what to do with my sad story of a life, I'll watch more video footage.

I'm twenty minutes in, watching the camera feeds at five times the normal speed. Brandy has been in the office for almost ten minutes searching high and low, and I'll give you one guess what she's looking for—that ring of Boone's I've been meaning to give back. She'll never find it, though.

Finally, someone else steps into the bar. Brandy bolts from the little back room so fast, you'd have thought her ass was on fire.

Oh God. Please, no. I can't watch this.

My stomach twists and cramps with each passing second as the feed plays on, and sinks to my feet as I watch a hand fling out and catch Brandy's face high on her cheekbone.

Oh. Shit. I can feel the smack like it landed on my own face.

Brandy shrinks back again like she's expecting another

blow, but it doesn't come. Finally, she's alone, leaning on the bar, her head bowed and shoulders shaking.

I flip the laptop lid closed, the sick feeling twisting in my gut even stronger.

How am I going to turn this in?

I don't have a choice. I have to.

If there was any chance at salvaging what Boone and I were building, it's gone. Brandy made sure of it.

It was never going to last, especially not with the odds stacked against us.

My eyes burn with tears that I refuse to let fall.

Stop it, Ripley. You could never have him anyway. It's not like you can lose something that wasn't yours to begin with.

And he wasn't. Won't be. Ever.

Now more than ever, I want to go straight to the cops so I don't have to face Boone and admit why he was arrested, but I talk myself out of it. I might be the unluckiest girl in Nashville, but I still have a backbone. I'm a coward if I don't face him and give him the evidence he needs to be vindicated. Then the world will have its proof that Boone didn't do what Brandy said he did.

And in doing so, I'm doing the unthinkable.

I stand and straighten my shoulders, tight from being hunched over while watching the tape.

I don't have another choice. This is the only one I can make and still live with myself.

Boone doesn't deserve to suffer for my family's problems. No, he deserves the best life has to offer—and we all know that isn't Ripley Fischer.

CHAPTER EIGHT

BOONE

A nthony and I are turning down the driveway at my place, trying to come up with a strategy based on all the shit the lawyers have told me, when he slams on the brakes to avoid running into a rusted Javelin parked in front of the gate.

"What the hell?" Anthony says.

"It's Ripley. Let her in."

"No shit."

Anthony hits a remote hooked to the visor and the gate swings open. He gives the horn a double tap, indicating that she should go first, and Ripley's car lurches forward in a way that makes me think her transmission is about to die.

Logan Brantley could make that car purr like a kitten and growl like a bitch, just like he did for my 442.

We follow Ripley up the drive, and she parks off to the side of the garage when Anthony pulls inside. I'm out of the SUV in less than two seconds.

After the pictures of Amber and me hit the Internet, I knew there was a chance Ripley might bail. Most people don't stop to ask questions with that shit; they just jump to conclusions and assume the worst.

But not my girl. She's better than that.

I catch sight of her as she climbs out of the Javelin and shuts the door.

Maybe I'm wrong. Her face is pale and drawn, and the dark circles under her eyes tell me she didn't sleep last night.

Maybe she was worried about me? I told her to stay at my place, but obviously she didn't, and now she looks like she'd rather be anywhere else.

But Ripley's not looking at me. She's looking at the SUV behind me . . . as if expecting someone else to follow.

She glances at the ground and then back to the car door again, and that's when it hits me. *She's waiting for Amber to get out.*

"Just you and me and Anthony, sugar," I say, answering her unspoken question.

I know she wants to ask where Amber is, but I'm way more interested in what brought Ripley to my gate if she expected to find me back with my ex. She's not spitting fire, so an ass-ripping doesn't appear to be the answer.

Still, she doesn't speak, and standing twenty feet away from her while she's hugging something to her chest and looking broken and lost is more than I can take. I cross the pavement and am about to pull her into my arms when she holds something out in front of her like a shield. Or an offering.

A laptop.

"I have proof."

"What?"

"Proof that you didn't touch Brandy and someone else did."

I look at the laptop and then up at her face. "How?"

"I installed security cameras at the bar. Just some cheap DIY ones that send the feeds to a server offsite, and I can watch it on my computer. Brandy didn't know. Pop didn't know. Just me. I wanted to catch her hand in the till so I knew where all my profits were going."

"No shit." Anthony says the words on a breath of relief.

"You need to see this. Give it to the cops. They'll have to drop the charges. She can't lie about it anymore."

"Does she know you have this?"

This question also comes from Anthony because I'm too busy studying all the features of Ripley's face, trying to figure out why she's doing this if she expected Amber to get out of the car behind me.

Ripley shakes her head. "No. She doesn't have a clue."

"That's a goddamned miracle."

It's like Ripley and Anthony are holding a conversation without me being present, because I'm still working out what I want to say.

I reach out to brush my thumb across Ripley's cheek, but she flinches and draws back. Her reaction tells me everything I need to know.

I step away, and Anthony comes toward us. "Can I get a look at the footage? We need to get the ball rolling."

"Let's go inside, and we can all check it out." There's no emotion in my voice because it's all balled up, burning a hole in my chest. *She flinched and stepped away.*

I spin on the heel of my boot and lead the way through the garage and into the house. Anthony follows and Ripley trails behind him. In the kitchen, we wait while she sets up the laptop on the counter. It's a model so ancient, I'm surprised it still works.

When she hits PLAY, we watch the screen in silence. First, me arguing with Brandy, and then Ripley skips forward. Anthony and I wince when the blow is delivered.

"Shit," Anthony says under his breath.

I look at Ripley, whose face is even paler now than it was when she was in the driveway. "Who is that?" I ask.

Her voice is quiet when she replies. "My dad."

CHAPTER
NINE

RIPLEY

B oth men go silent after my confession, and I wonder what they're thinking. Probably *how could he hit a woman?*

The answer I'll never give? *Easy. He's been doing it for years.*

They're both staring at the screen when I hit PAUSE and step away. I wrap both arms around my middle. I feel like I'm being torn in two as I hand them the tool to destroy what's left of my family, but I have no choice. Pop brought this on himself. For years, he's gotten away with no consequences. Brandy too. Still, handing someone the hammer to nail the coffin shut after being loyal for so long is harder than I thought it would be.

I have no choice. Boone didn't ask for any of this. My family tried to destroy his reputation, and all he did . . . was be nice to me.

I'm a pariah. It's time to wrap this up and get the hell away from Boone before I do any more damage.

"You can keep the laptop. I don't need it right now. Show

the police. You can show the media if you need to." The words are rusty, as if my throat is trying to keep them in, but there's no use. Pop made his bed, and now he has to lie in it.

Anthony turns to Boone. "I gotta make some calls right now. I got a buddy on the force, and even though he's not working this case, he'll be able to tell us exactly how we should go about bringing this in. We need to handle this right." He gives us both a nod before striding away, leaving Boone and me alone.

I can barely bring myself to look him in the eye, but I find my spine and straighten my shoulders.

"I'm sorry doesn't come close to being a decent apology, but it's all I've got right now. You didn't deserve any of it. And I'm so freaking sorry that my disaster of a family pulled you into our mess. You deserve so much better." I swallow back the lump in my throat. "I'll get Hope's truck, and we'll take Esteban as soon as we can."

At his name, Esteban wakes in the living room. *"Take me away."*

I take a step in his direction, but Boone's fingers lock around my wrist.

"I'm not back with her."

I swing my head around in his direction as he continues.

"If you saw the pictures from earlier, it was all a stunt by Amber. I didn't have shit to do with it. She and I are done, Ripley. I swear it on my granddad's grave."

A spark of something unfamiliar grows in my mind, maybe hope, but I refuse to give it any fuel to grow. *Regardless of whether he's back with Amber, Boone and I are done. This can't go anywhere.*

"It doesn't matter, Boone. My family—"

He tugs me back, never releasing his hold on me. "Your family isn't you. You didn't pick them. You didn't do shit. They've treated you like crap for years and you're still here, doing the right thing, but struggling with that family loyalty all the same."

I shake my head. "You don't understand. I have the world's worst luck. If something can go wrong for me, it will. This is just one more example of why you need to stay far away from me. I'd never forgive myself if I dragged you down with me."

With another swift tug, Boone brings me flush against his body, and I don't have the emotional strength to fight it. If this is the last time I get to be close to him, I need to soak it up. I'll drag out this memory when I'm alone, and remember what it was like to have someone like Boone care.

"I forgive you, even though there's nothing to forgive," Boone says, his voice low and quiet, his gaze drilling into mine. "I won't let them keep you out of my life." He releases my wrist and his hand slides around to the small of my back. "We're just getting started, sugar, and I won't let anyone take that away from us."

I try to pull back because his words are all too perfect, designed to make me agree with anything he wants from me, but I can't buy into it. He doesn't understand.

"You don't get it, Boone. This can't go anywhere." My voice shakes, and I know I'm about to lose it.

"Who says it can't go anywhere?" His posture goes rigid.

"Me! Things don't work out for me. Ever. I *never* get a break. Every time I think maybe something is gonna go right, life smacks me down again, just to put me in my place. Ripley Fischer thought she could have something better? Nope. Not a chance. Let's make sure that goes to shit too."

His expression softens. "What are you talking about, sugar?"

"Life, Boone! Not everything works out just because you want it to. If something can go wrong, it will. Maybe not for everyone, but for me, that's how it works."

"That's bullshit." His blue eyes spark.

"No, that's the truth. I spent years avoiding getting involved with someone like you, someone with cameras and paparazzi following them everywhere, because of what happened with my mama. She hooked up with Gil Green, and then the next thing you know, they're both dead. Pop never missed an opportunity to hammer me with what Mama did, and how the apple doesn't fall far from the tree. And then on top of all that, I know I have the world's shit-tiest luck, and I *still* let myself get involved with you against my better judgment. Now look at the freaking mess you're in! It's not just the press calling me a whore, but my cousin lied to the police and got you thrown in jail! Oh, and on top of that, your girlfriend comes back and rescues you. How much more proof do you need?"

"Nothing happened with Amber—"

I laugh, and it comes out sounding maniacal. "I believe you. I really, truly do. But guess what? It doesn't matter what I think, because the rest of the world believes what they read online and in the tabloids. And that just *sucks*. I don't even know why I'm surprised. *I never get a break.*" My voice rises and I sound hysterical, even to my own ears. "I let myself think for a second that maybe this could go right. Maybe I could finally have something good in my life, and look how royally it got screwed up. So I'm done. Just . . .

done. I give up. I'm going to walk away before anything else bad can happen. I'll be back for my bird, but that's it."

Boone's face morphs into a harsh mask. "You had exactly one part right—this is a good thing going between us, and that hasn't fucking changed. We hit a few bumps in the road, but everyone does. If you expect life to be perfect, then you're not living it right."

"Perfect?" I laugh. "Not even—"

Boone throws up a hand and interrupts. "You had your say, and now it's my turn to talk, sugar. So listen up. What we've got isn't over. Not even close. You can tell me all day long that you never get a break and nothing ever goes right for you, but I'm here to tell you that this is very right."

I shake my head. "You can feed me a line, Boone, but I'm not buying it. Girls like me don't get happily-ever-afters."

"I'm just gonna have to prove you wrong then."

I should tell him there's not a chance in hell, but instead I whisper, "I don't expect anything from you. No expectations is the only way I can put one foot in front of the other anymore. Anything else just leads to more disappointment than I can handle."

Boone reaches out and grasps my hips, hauling me close to his body. His lips ghost alongside my temple, and I swear he's breathing me in.

"What if I want you to expect things from me? What if I promise I'm not going to disappoint you?" He pulls back and those blue eyes lock onto mine.

Self-preservation is screaming *tell him you can't take the chance*. But another voice, a stupid one, is yelling *don't you dare tell him no*.

Anthony bursts into the room, talking a mile a minute.

"Boone, I just talked to my buddy. He said we gotta get

this shit down to the station ASA-fucking-P. They need to log it into evidence and get it in front of the judge. He says the charges could be dropped before the end of the day. There's a good chance that Brandy could be charged with filing a false police report too. Cops don't like it when they fuck up big in this kind of case, so they'll need to cover their asses. And once they see this, they'll probably be picking up the old man and asking if she wants to press charges against him." He stops when he finally reaches us. "Shit. That's your dad. I didn't mean any disrespect."

I step back and look away from Boone's intense stare, thankful for the reprieve. I was on the edge of doing something too stupid for consideration. I need to get out of here.

"It's okay. I have to go. I need to get back to Hope's to change for work and head in for my shift."

Boone's gaze drops to my feet. My ankle, actually. "You shouldn't be standing for an eight-hour shift." His expression turns rueful when he meets my eyes again. "But you know that already."

My posture stiffens and I cross my arms. "I need this job, and I'm not going to make Hope look bad by bailing again right after she hired me."

"You're not bailing—"

I hold up a hand, and shockingly, Boone goes silent. "I need to find another place to live and sort out my life. And both of those cost money, which requires a job."

His blue eyes blaze even hotter now than they did moments ago. I can tell he wants to argue with me, but he doesn't.

What Hope asked me earlier comes back. *What do I want to do? Who do I want to be?*

I still don't have an answer, but I know that couch-surfing on her futon isn't it. I want to be able to take care of myself and weather storms as they come. I don't want to be dependent on anyone for a handout. My pride has taken a beating lately, and I'd like to keep a few shreds of it intact.

"Just . . . take it easy tonight, sugar. I got a vested interest in making sure you're whole and healthy."

Boone's words wrap around me, and a warm feeling glows in my chest. *Don't get used to it*, I order myself.

"I'll be fine." I turn away, glancing at Esteban as an excuse. He's watching us both silently, which isn't normal for him.

"*Crackerhead*," he squawks before lifting one wing.

"I'll be back for him as soon as I can."

A smooth smile slides across Boone's face. "You think I won't hold the bird hostage? You don't know me very well then, sugar. No matter what you think, we're just getting started."

CHAPTER TEN

RIPLEY

"We need someone to test the sound system," Hope says as I slide behind the bar, ready to work. "Want to go put it through its paces?"

I glance around the mostly empty bar. Only a few people are drinking this early, and most of the staff are still getting ready for the place to open.

"You mean like, 'Testing, one, two'?" I ask her.

Hope grins. "I sure as hell don't. You know exactly what I mean. It's open-mic night. We need to make sure someone with surprising pipes doesn't blow out our eardrums if there's feedback."

Bartenders who can sing are a dime a dozen in this town, so I know I'm nothing special, but even so, I never do it in public. When Gil Green gave me that pink kid's guitar twenty years ago, I would stand onstage at the Fishbowl when Pop wasn't around and belt out my favorite Patsy Cline and Reba songs. Mama would clap and yell for an encore, but once we heard any sound that indicated Pop was coming back, the guitar would get hidden away until it was safe again.

When Mama died, any aspirations my nine-year-old self had died with her. I still played the chords on that guitar, but I never stepped onstage and pretended to perform again. After the way the press dragged my family through the mud, I never wanted to be in the spotlight. *And I've done a great job screwing that up lately.*

But this one time . . . it can't hurt anything. I might be a little rusty from only singing in the shower or my car, but why not? A thrill zips through me as I remember how much I loved playing and singing for Mama.

I scan the bar again. Eight people. Safe enough.

Hope grins like she knows she's won.

"Fine. I'll do it. You gonna pick?" I almost regret asking, because I wouldn't put it past her to suggest something crazy.

"Nah, give it a go with whatever."

I cross toward the stage where the sound crew set up everything for open-mic night instead of the house band instruments. This is about one voice and whatever instrument the person brings with them. As I step up onto the raised platform, I wonder if anyone has ever been discovered at the White Horse. It has been a fixture in Nashville for years, so it wouldn't surprise me, but the chances have to be slim to none. *And also completely irrelevant.* I'm a bartender, not a nine-year-old with a pipe dream.

I take the microphone off the stand with a sweaty hand and flip it on. I go through the usual round of "Testing, one, two" anyway, and Hope gives me a thumbs-up from the bar.

Now what? I lean back, resting my butt on the tall stool in the middle of the stage. A song that has run through my brain so many times over the last few years rushes back to me. I can picture the video of the girl fighting with her drunk of a father, wishing a tornado would blow it all away.

Very fitting, so I launch into Carrie Underwood's "Blown Away."

I'm probably crazy to sing it *a cappella*, but in this moment, I don't give two shits what anyone thinks. The song and the story wrap around me and transport me somewhere else, on the outside looking in on all those times my father told me I wasn't good enough. All the times he called my mother a whore and told me I was just like her.

I just want it all to blow away.

But unlike the song, there's not enough rain in Nashville to wipe the sins from that bar. It will never be clean again.

I lose myself in the lyrics, belting them out with everything I have, not caring if I'm off-key, because I feel every last word down to my soul.

When I whisper the last *away*, I finally open my eyes. The bar is silent. Every single person in the room is on their feet, their mouths agape, staring at me.

One of the waitresses starts a slow clap, and everyone else joins in as someone yells *encore!*

A rush of heat burns my cheeks as I realize I just bared my soul onstage in front of a room of strangers. I flip off the mic and shove it back in the stand before giving them a nod and stepping off the platform.

People are smiling and clapping as I walk by.

"Holy shit, girl. You got *pipes*."

"Damn, I did *not* see that coming!"

"Why are you serving drinks instead of playing shows?"

I smile at them as the comments come, but hurry back behind the bar where I feel safer. When I get there, Hope says nothing, choosing to watch me with a smug smile as I grab a towel and unnecessarily wipe down the bar.

"Sound system works fine," I mumble.

When I came in today, I told her everything that happened with Boone. She listened until I finished, then wrapped me in a tight hug and whispered, "It sucks now, but I promise it's going to get better." She knew I needed this outlet to pour out my frustrations and disappointments, and set them free.

"I'd say it's never worked better," she deadpans.

"Stop it." I'm fighting a smile. I don't want to admit just how good that felt, because I can still feel eyes on me. After my little performance, I don't need to draw any more attention to myself.

Apparently, that ship has sailed.

"Well, shit. You could've been filling that bar of yours every night of the week if you'd just stepped on your own damn stage, Rip."

I jerk my head around to see Zane Frisco staring at me, his hand wrapped around a beer and a broad smile on his face.

Oh crap. Where did he come from?

"I don't perform," I tell him.

He lifts the beer to his lips and tips back a swig. He doesn't speak again until he lowers it to the bar. "So, what the hell would you call that? Oh, wait, we could call it God-given talent going to waste."

I grab a towel and wipe down the perfectly clean section in front of me, needing to be doing something with my hands. Hope heads to the end of the bar where a customer waits, which officially steals my best excuse for escaping.

I finally look up at Frisco. "Please don't say anything. No

one needs to know. It's not a big deal."

His thumb skims along the lip of his pint glass, wiping away the condensation as I wait impatiently for him to say something, preferably that he'll keep his trap shut. What he says instead sends ice through my veins.

"If you think that someone in here didn't record at least part of that and post it on YouTube already, then you're more naive than I realized."

My gaze cuts away from Frisco and darts from person to person in the bar, as if a sign might pop up above someone's head saying I DID IT. MY ASS IS THE ONE YOU NEED TO KICK. Obviously, that doesn't happen.

As an alternative, I decide to go with denial. "No one would do that. It was . . . nothing."

Frisco huffs out a mocking laugh. "Sure thing, Rip. We'll just call it nothing." His eyes lift to meet mine. "It's better than calling it bullshit."

"Wait, what?" The accusation has me jerking back.

Frisco's easy demeanor dissipates. "*Bullshit,*" he repeats. "Because you've been hiding the fact that you could be opening concerts and working your way up to stadium shows right alongside me and the other assholes in this town trying to make it, and you're over here pretending it's nothing. You know how many people would kill to have that talent? Hundreds. Fuck, thousands." His hands curl into fists on the bar on either side of his drink. "Instead, you're spending your best years buried behind a bar. What a fucking waste."

The anger in his voice hits me hard in the chest, and I shoot back in kind.

"You don't get to decide what's a waste and what's not. There are probably thousands of people out there with more natural talent than me who aren't using it, so why don't you go feed them this line of crap? You've got no say on how I live my life, Frisco, so don't even start."

His voice drops, going low and rough. "You know why I'm here, Ripley? You think this was my dream? Hustling my way through Nashville, trying to make it? No. It was my sister's dream, and she wanted it more than anything. More ambition than talent and common sense combined. She bought into some asshole's line about how they could make her famous, and the next thing I know, she's not singing for her supper, she's fucking for it." His furious gaze tears into me. "I came here to find her. Ready to tear this city apart, if that's what it took to bring her home. But it was too fucking late. She was gone. My twin. Twenty-two and dead."

The ferocity in his voice is only outweighed by the pain.

"I stayed because music was the only outlet I had. I threw myself into it, and somehow I got the lucky break she didn't. Now I live with the guilt every damn day."

"I'm so sorry, Frisco. I had no idea."

He lifts his pint glass to his lips and chugs the beer, smacking the bottom against the wood when he finishes.

"Yeah, well, shit happens. But you got talent, and the fact that you're wasting it slinging drinks pisses me the fuck off. Now I'm gonna stay perched on this fucking stool all night and get hammered. My babysittin' abilities are gonna be impaired, but if shit goes down, I'll definitely be ready to throw some punches."

I'm still absorbing all his words, and one stands out at me. *Babysitting?*

Boone.

"He asked you to come keep an eye on me?"

I don't even have to say his name for Frisco to nod. We

both know exactly who I'm talking about. But why? A rush of confusion blows through me, and I have to ask it aloud.

"Why?" My question produces an *are you frigging stupid* look from Frisco, but no response. There's another subject I need to bring up, but right now isn't exactly the best time. Then again, I can't let it lie any longer. "You know it wasn't personal, me turning you down when you'd come into the Fishbowl, right?"

Frisco's grip on his drink tightens. "Yeah, your rule lasted about thirty seconds after you met Boone, but I'm a big enough man not to hold it against you."

"I know I owe you an explanation, but I really can't—"

He holds up his other hand, and I go silent. "You don't have to explain shit to me, Rip. You win some, you lose some. That's how the game goes. Now, I'm ready for another beer."

He shoves his empty glass toward me, and I can't bring myself to keep pushing. He's already torn up and raw from his confession about his sister, and I'm just adding insult to injury.

I retrieve the pint. "Your usual?"

"Yeah."

"I'll get you another."

"Much appreciated."

I flip the tap and let the glass fill with Bud before sliding it back in front of him, keeping my fingers wrapped around it when he tries to take it from me. After a beat, Frisco meets my gaze.

"I'm truly sorry for everything, especially about your sister. It's not fair. I know exactly how much it sucks to lose someone before their time." And because my emotions are flowing tonight, I add, "My mama sang. She wanted to be a star too, but Pop wouldn't let her step foot onstage after they got together. That's probably why she liked all those celebrities coming into the bar back in the day. I think it was her way of living vicariously through them because she'd never get the chance herself. I'll always wonder what would have happened if she'd left Pop and gone out on her own, instead of . . ."

I trail off as understanding dawns in Frisco's eyes.

"If Pop had known I could sing and had any ambition in that direction, he would've been even more cruel than normal. I think I knew that, even as a kid. So I buried it, because it doesn't make sense to have a dream when you know there's no chance of it ever coming true."

Frisco's expression softens. "You're not under your old man's thumb anymore, and you can't know whether it's gonna come true or not until you try."

I blink away a few drops of unexpected moisture gathering in the corners of my eyes. I refuse to call them tears.

"You're right, but at the moment, the only thing I need in my life is reality, not dreams. I need a paycheck so I can get my shit together. Maybe when I'm not sleeping on my best friend's futon anymore, I'll let myself do a little dreaming."

"Fair enough. Sorry I snapped at you, Rip. It's a tough subject for me."

"I understand. No apologies necessary, Frisco. I'll keep the beers coming."

I move down the bar to take more orders, but in the back of my mind, I'm stuck on the fact that Boone asked Frisco to watch out for me. *When's the last time anyone cared enough to do something like that?*

It doesn't matter. It's not happening.

But I can't deny the warmth buzzing through my veins.

CHAPTER ELEVEN

RIPLEY

It doesn't take long for word to spread about my impromptu performance. Frisco obviously has more experience than I do with this. The video is already up on YouTube, and while it hasn't gone viral, I know from Hope's repeated checking that it's getting more hits than I'm comfortable with. While I sling drinks and voice after voice comes through the open mic, plenty of people come to the bar and wave their phones in my face, asking *is this you?*

I pretend I can't hear them over the music and ask for their drink order.

Working my way down the bar, I stop in front of the stool where Frisco has been parked all night, but an unfamiliar face looks up at me.

Where did he go?

I take the man's order as Frisco's voice comes over the speakers.

"I know I've been crashing here a little too often, but it's just 'cause I like y'all. Whatcha want to hear? I feel like doing a cover."

The energy changes in the White Horse like someone flipped a switch. People scream out requests, and I have to believe it's no accident that Frisco chooses one of Boone's songs.

"Shit. This place is going to turn into a madhouse again now that he's onstage. Get ready for it, girl." Hope hip checks me as she passes by with an armful of mixers to restock.

"I'm ready. Bring it."

I make drinks, getting lost in Frisco's voice and Boone's words. When Frisco finishes, the crowd screams and shouts, and he waits for them to quiet down before speaking into the microphone again. What he says next almost stops my heart.

"What about doing something a little different before I give up the mic to the next person in line? I've got a good friend here, and she can sing. I think it's time for a duet, don't you, Ripley Fischer?"

I'm gonna kill him. I felt bad for him an hour ago, but now I'm gonna kill him.

Frisco starts the crowd chanting "Rip-ley, Rip-ley," but I don't move from behind the bar until Hope stops beside me again.

"Well, you gonna go?"

I shake my head.

"Why not?"

"Because! I don't—"

"Come on, Ripley. We're all waiting for you."

I cover my face with a hand, but unless I duck out the back, there's no getting out of this.

"Just go. It'll be fine." Hope sounds like she thinks this is a good idea.

I might need to murder my best friend too.

I tug out the bar towel tucked into the back pocket of my jeans and drop it on the counter.

"I'm going to regret this, aren't I?"

Hope's lips turn up in a smile. "You only regret the chances you don't take. Go for it, girl. Cat's already out of the bag, so what's the harm?"

You only regret the chances you don't take . . . God, I hope she's right.

With a steadying breath, I slide out from behind the bar, and the crowd parts to make a path to the stage. My nerves are stretched to the limit as people start to clap and cheer and yell my name.

Oh God. What if I suck? I've never done a duet. This is the worst idea ever.

The voice in my head that loves to play devil's advocate pipes up. *Or it could be the first step in a completely new direction. Take a chance. What do you have to lose?*

With conflict raging inside me, I climb onto the stage. Frisco winks at me and wraps an arm around my shoulders, turning me so I face the crowd.

"Give it up for Ripley Fischer, y'all!"

I plaster a smile on my face and hope they can't tell I'm terrified. When I meet Frisco's eyes, he lowers the mic and puts his mouth to my ear.

"I know you want to kill me right now, but sometimes it takes a push in the right direction to realize your dreams are worth chasing."

CHAPTER
TWELVE

RIPLEY

The lyrics from the duet Frisco and I sang at the White Horse are still streaming through my mind the next afternoon.

A Great Big World and Christina Aguilera's "Say Something." It wasn't exactly country, but I followed Frisco's lead after he dragged a keyboard onstage, and it was insane.

Every time one of us would say "I'm giving up on you," a shaft of pain would stab through me. Even though I know it's the right thing to do with Boone, the ache hasn't subsided.

Maybe if I were one of those people who were all about the power of positive thinking, I would believe Boone's vow that he's going to change my mind. But we all know positive thinking isn't exactly my forte, and at this point, I'm not sure if I can handle more disappointment.

I'm giving up on you.

It's the safest thing I could do and the only way I can protect myself. But am I ready to say good-bye?

I don't know what possesses me to go surfing the gossip

sites, but I do it anyway. Maybe just to drive home the fact that anything else isn't an option at this point.

The headlines assail me as I click on the first link.

AMBER FLEET AND BOONE THRASHER REPAIRING WHAT'S BROKEN?

There's a picture of Boone and Amber at Home Depot standing in front of a tool aisle, and it's dated today. I scan the article, and although it doesn't say they were spotted together and this is a new picture, the writer implies that's the case.

No way. He wouldn't.

I don't know why I'm so sure he wouldn't, but I have to know I'm right.

On my laptop, I can do a reverse Google image search, but I don't know how on my phone. Instead, I pull up Google and search *Boone Thrasher Amber Fleet Home Depot*.

The same picture pops up in an article dated over a year ago, and a rush of relief washes over me—at least until I slam headfirst into a mental wall.

Why am I doing this to myself?

I don't know, but I can't help it. I keep scanning until I see an article with a picture of Amber holding up lingerie in some fancy-looking boutique that I couldn't afford to step foot inside, let alone buy a pair of panties. I guess it's a good thing I don't wear them. Still, the headline makes me throw up a little in my mouth.

COUNTRY STARLET PLANS TO TAKE BACK HER MAN

I snort and think, *He doesn't want you back, bitch. He wants me. Whatcha gonna do about it?*

Then I catch myself. *What am I doing?* I need to be searching for apartments and doing something useful, like finding a second job I can work during the day so I can get on my feet faster.

Then my cell phone rings, obscuring the picture of perfect Amber and her perfect freaking lingerie.

Hope.

"Hey, what's going on?" I ask. "Everything okay?"

She had a doctor's appointment this morning for her annual, which reminds me I really need to get on it and do the same.

"Yeah, fine. I just stopped into work to pick up something, and there are a ton of voice mails from people asking about you."

"What?" I shriek the word and it echoes through the empty apartment.

"Yeah, agents, some label scouts. They all want the name of the girl who either *sang that Carrie song* or *rocked the duet with Zane Frisco.*"

"No way."

"Have you been online today at all?"

I lie. "Um, no. Why?"

"Your video with Frisco is *everywhere*. I mean, we're talking almost a quarter of a million hits, and it's not stopping there."

I know you can't technically tell when all the blood

drains from your face, but the tingling sensation in my cheeks leads me to believe that's exactly what's happening. Or maybe it's the way my stomach is flopping like a fish.

I drop onto the futon, a second from putting my head between my legs. "No way."

"Yes, way. Girl, your whole life might've just changed. I know you said you didn't know what you wanted to do, but this might have decided that for you."

"That's impossible. I mean, I . . . I can't. That's not—"

"Calm down, Rip. It's only if you want it. You know these things build for a while, and then they die out eventually if nothing else comes of it . . . but you need to give it some serious thought before you dismiss it. This could be huge. A chance to live that dream you've buried. For you and . . ." She trails off, but I know what she wants to say.

For me and my mama.

My response is to stay silent, because words have deserted me.

"Think about it, Rip. This might be life handing you exactly what you need, when you need it."

My grip on the phone tightens. "Thank you for telling me. I'll think about it."

I can tell she wants to say more, but instead she whispers, "Love you, girl."

"Love you too."

When we hang up, I open my browser again and search for *Zane Frisco duet.*

The results load in a half second.

Holy Jesus. It's on dozens of sites, and Hope's right. The YouTube hits are still steadily climbing.

Oh God. This is really happening.

Then another thought slams into me. *How long until they*

connect it to the girl who supposedly broke up Boone's engagement?

I groan and flop back onto the futon. I need coffee. A whole boatload of coffee.

After sneaking down to the corner coffee shop the next morning in a baseball cap and sunglasses to hide the dark circles under my eyes from a restless night and the rat's nest of my hair, I see a handful of people gathered in small groups in the seating area.

No one looks at me twice, and for that I'm thankful, because I'm being nosy and see the video of the duet on at least one screen.

I get my coffee and get the hell out of there. I'm halfway up the stairs to Hope's apartment when my cell phone rings. Balancing my coffee and muffin in one hand, I pull my phone out of my pocket.

Zane Frisco.

I answer by saying, "Oh my God. What the hell did you do?"

"Me? You were part of it too, girl. And everyone's going crazy over this shit. I was trying to sleep in, but my phone wouldn't stop. My agent's already looking into what needs to happen to get us into the studio together to record the cover."

I lose my grip on the muffin and it bounces down the stairs. "What are you talking about? You told him I don't sing, didn't you?"

Frisco laughs. "It's kinda hard to tell him that when he saw the video."

"You know what I mean. I don't sing like *that*. It was just a one-time deal. I'm a bartender, not a wannabe country star."

"I hate to break it to you, Rip, but you're not a wannabe anything. Right now, you can actually be whatever you want. Not everyone gets that chance."

I know he's talking about his sister, and guilt is like a shiv in my gut.

"This is the opportunity of a lifetime. You sure you want to shut the door on it without even giving it a shot?"

I sit down on the stairs, not caring that the worn carpet has seen better days. "I don't know. This isn't something I expected to be worrying about this morning, okay? I have no idea how to respond."

"All I'm saying is you should give it some consideration before you shut it down. Thousands of people would kill for this kind of exposure, and if you think for a second you might want to try out this life, then you have to take it. It's not going to wait around for you. Right now, you're a mystery. A hot new sound everyone wants to get their hands on. If you wait too long, they'll move on to the next new thing."

I know what Frisco is saying is true, but didn't I just decide yesterday that every time I try to reach for something, I get smacked down? If I took this opportunity and it all went south, how humiliating would that be?

I was afraid to start something with Boone because I knew it would throw me into the spotlight, but wouldn't this do the same? And if I fail, there's no one else to blame. It's all on me.

"I get what you're saying, but I can't decide right now. I'm sitting on the stairs, wishing I had another muffin because mine plopped facedown at the bottom of the landing. You gotta give me a minute."

Frisco's quiet laugh comes over the line. "All right, Rip. Go get another muffin and think about it. You work today?"

"Yeah, at six."

"Don't be surprised if you're mobbed for more than drinks."

"I'm not too worried. Behind a bar, I blend in like furniture."

"You're totally friggin' wrong about that. I saw you clear as day, and Boone sure did too."

For a second I wonder if Frisco is still annoyed that I hooked up with Boone after I shut him down, but the tone of his voice is good natured.

"You sure you're not holding that against me? That I—"

"That you picked him and not me? Nah, I've got a big enough ego that I can handle it."

"Now that, I actually believe." I hesitate but ask the question that's on the tip of my tongue, even though I know I shouldn't. "Have you heard from him?"

"Nope. I'm a little surprised about it. You?"

"No."

"That's interesting."

"Why?"

"Shit. Sorry, Rip, I gotta go. Think about what I said."

He hangs up, and I'm left wondering why it's interesting Boone hasn't contacted either of us.

CHAPTER THIRTEEN

RIPLEY

I slam my palms on my steering wheel.

"Why? Why would you do this *today?* Come on!"

My Javelin is dead. She turned over once, sputtered, and went quiet, and now I can't get her to cough up a sound. And it's not because I ran out of gas again.

"Come on, girl. Just one more time."

I turn the key and pump the gas pedal, but nothing happens.

"Shit." I rest my forehead on the wheel for a moment.

Why me?

When there are no answers, which there never are, I suck it up and climb out of the car. I have fifteen minutes to get to work, and it looks like I'm walking—and adding *new car* to the list of things I need to save up to buy.

With a deep breath, I shove my keys in my bag. At least my shoes are comfortable for the sake of my ankle and the long shift ahead.

When I think about my ankle, it twinges a little with

each step. I've done my best to ignore it, and found that pretending it doesn't exist is the best pain relief out there.

Avoidance. Imagine that.

I'm about three blocks from Hope's apartment, walking toward Broadway, when a rumbling truck slows beside me. With a single glance, I know who it is.

He shoves the passenger door open from the inside. "Looks like you could use a ride."

Boone's familiar voice is almost enough to break me right now. Once again, things have gone to shit, and he's got a front-row seat. *Great.*

When I keep walking, focusing on putting one foot in front of the other, the truck inches forward next to me.

"Come on, sugar. Let me help you out."

I take a deep breath and slowly release it before climbing into Boone's big black truck.

"Thanks," I say without meeting his eyes.

"I was in the neighborhood. No big deal."

Awkwardsauce . . .

I clutch my bag on my lap and stare straight out the windshield as he flips off someone who honks at him before he accelerates again. I want to ask him if the charges have been dropped, but before I can form the question, he starts talking.

"Javelin finally gave up the ghost?"

"I'm hoping it's more along the lines of a temporary setback."

Boone's gaze cuts to me. "Temporary setback. Got it. So you need me to take a look at it and see what's going on?"

That's exactly what I need, but asking for help still isn't my strong suit. Then again, I also have no idea who to call that won't rip me off. The last time she played dead, I had a guy come out and charge me four hundred dollars to tell me there was nothing he could do. I didn't have the extra money to throw away then, and I sure don't have it now.

"Do you know anyone good?"

He nods. "Best guy is down in Kentucky. He could make her run like she just rolled off the line. Actually, probably better. He did my 442."

I think of the beautiful muscle car that Boone drives, and know instantly that his guy is totally out of my budget. "How about someone close and cheap?"

"I'll find someone."

"If you don't, it's no big deal. I can handle it—"

"Yourself?" Boone finishes for me. "You're one of the most capable women I've ever met, so I'm sure you could. But sometimes, you gotta accept a little help." He nods down at my ankle, reminding me that I accepted his help before and it turned out okay.

Okay? The orgasms at his house were more than okay.

I've tried to forget how his hands felt on my body, and how his mouth—

Stop. Don't go there. My admonition doesn't help, and now my nipples are hard, and I'm pretending I'm not thinking about what it would be like if Boone put this truck in park and yanked me onto his lap.

Ahh. Stop. I shut down that line of thinking just in time for Boone to pull up behind the White Horse. I reach for the door handle of the truck.

"Thanks for the ride. I appreciate it."

Before I can escape, he hits a button and I'm trapped. I jerk my head to look at him.

"What the hell?"

"Child locks."

"Yeah, I get that. Now let me out." To myself I add, *Before I do something stupid, like throw myself at you.*

Boone crosses his arms and his expression turns determined. "You're not gettin' out of this truck until you tell me you're not giving up on us. I saw the video of you and Frisco. I know the song. If that was supposed to be some kind of message to me, I'm saying *no fucking way*. I told you we're not done. We've barely gotten started. Now I need to know that you get me."

"It was just a song."

"Bullshit." The word comes out with a sharp edge. "You want to feed that line to someone else, go right ahead, but I perform for a living and I know when an artist feels the lyrics they're singing."

"It wasn't just about you. It was about me too."

Boone's blue eyes drill into mine. "And I have an even bigger problem with that. You're not giving up on yourself either. I won't let you."

"That's not a choice you get to make."

Boone grips the steering wheel with one hand, his frustration evident as his knuckles turn white.

"Give me a chance, Ripley. Just one goddamned chance to prove that this can work, that it can be the most beautiful thing you've ever had in your life."

The conviction behind his words knocks a few bricks from the wall I've built around my heart.

I want that. I want something beautiful. But I'm scared to believe him, and feel the sting of life ripping it away from me.

"I need to go to work. I can't afford to lose this job, Boone."

His lips compress into a thin, flat line and his nostrils

flare. "I'll pick you up at closing. You're not walking home."

"I'll get a ride. It's no big—"

"I'll be here to pick you up."

His tone leaves no room for argument, and the clock on the dash says I don't have any more time for it either. *And, dammit, I didn't get to ask him about the charges being dropped.*

"Fine."

Boone unlocks the door, and I open it and slide out.

Before I can shut it behind me, he asks, "You gettin' onstage again tonight?"

I shake my head. "It's not open-mic night. Why?"

"Because I want to hear that incredible voice of yours in person."

CHAPTER FOURTEEN

BOONE

I can do incognito. It's a skill you hone in this business, and tonight I'm putting it to work and walking into the White Horse unnoticed.

I'm not taking the chance that Ripley will get it into her head to be stubborn and walk home. I just found her, and there's no way I'm going to risk losing her.

Sitting at the bar, I glance at the stage, wishing I'd been here last night when the videos I saw on YouTube were recorded. Am I insanely proud that she can bring a crowd to its feet and hold them enthralled? Absolutely, even if it does complicate things.

Ripley isn't prepared in the least for what she'd be stepping into if she decides to take this opportunity and run with it. Shit, Nick even called me when he saw the video and said he'd think about signing her, because right now it would be so easy to get her a deal.

Nick's exact words? *"You can't make up a better backstory. Former bartender with a tragic past, discovered at open mic-night after capturing the attention of one of country music's biggest stars. Who wouldn't sign her?"*

But to me, Ripley can't be summed up that easily. She's so much more than they realize. Definitely more than she realizes.

I'm at the end of the bar Hope is working, but with my thicker beard, cowboy hat, and pearl-snap shirt, I look like another wannabe cowboy. It sucks to ditch my T-shirt and ball cap, but I'm willing to suck it up for one night of anonymity.

I keep my tattoos hidden in the shadows as I nurse a beer and watch Ripley hustle. Do I feel like a stalker? A little. But I choose to think of it as keeping an eye out to make sure she gets home safe.

More than one person has approached her, and I can tell when it's about last night's performances because her body language changes completely. She goes from customer-service mode to totally uncomfortable in a heartbeat.

She doesn't even realize she could probably have a record deal by next weekend if she wanted. *Likely with a crap label who's going to give her a shit deal.*

Unless . . . There's one label in town that's starting to make a reputation for itself as an artist's label—Homegrown Records. Holly Wix Karas wouldn't let it be anything less. If Ripley wants to do this right, Homegrown is the way to go.

I need to make a call. Just in case.

Now that Holly's back to work part-time after having the baby, I bet she'd be interested in picking up some new talent for her label, especially someone as down to earth as Ripley.

The more I think about it, there's no one else I'd feel as comfortable having her sign with, not even my own label.

I lower my beer when I realize where this train of thought has taken me.

It doesn't matter what I want or don't want for Ripley. All that matters is what she wants. And if she wants to run with this, I'll support her every step of the way and make sure she has every advantage.

CHAPTER FIFTEEN

RIPLEY

The crowd gets thicker as the night goes on, instead of thinning out like I hoped. I should be happy the tips are flowing, so I focus on that instead of the fact that my ankle is aching something fierce. Of course I forgot to grab some Advil to shove in my bag, and the first aid kit is out, so I'm gritting my teeth against the pain.

The bands booked for tonight weren't bad, but they also weren't great. Regardless, I've been thinking all night about what it would be like to be onstage instead of behind the bar. Standing up there gives you a completely different perspective. The crowd was so into the music, and when I let myself get sucked into the lyrics, it went so fast. Only a few minutes, but for each second, I was transported somewhere else. Away from the constant grind that has become my life.

Maybe everyone's right. Maybe this is my one shot, and I'd be a fool not to take it.

I move down the bar, taking orders and making drinks until I come face-to-face with my cousin.

"I'd order a double shot of revenge, but I hear that's best served cold." Brandy's tone carries a sharp edge of malice.

I wish I'd asked Boone what the hell had happened before I got out of the truck.

"You brought it on yourself."

The corners of her mouth turn down in a scowl. "You betrayed your own family. Who does that?"

I want to scream *you do* for all the times Brandy has screwed me over, but there are too many people watching for me to lose my shit.

"Say your piece and kindly leave. I'm working."

"Say my piece? Okay, I'll get right on that, *Ripley*." My name sounds like a curse on her lips. "How could you turn your back on the people who did so much for you? Me, your pop, my mom—"

Her twisted view of things makes me want to throw up. "Are you serious? Pop *fired* me and threw me out. You've been stealing from the bar. You're the reason I installed the stupid cameras to begin with. Then you sold me out to the media after one freaking night! And I haven't done a damn thing to your mom—"

Brandy laughs. "Wasn't my fault you weren't more careful with him. You're lucky I didn't do worse. Now I wish I'd taped all that grunting and moaning. I could've made a million off a sex tape. Easy."

Oh. My. God.

"You didn't," I breathe in horror, thinking what an absolute disaster that would be.

"No, but I should have. Now I've got no job, and they're saying if I can't pay the fine, they'll send me to jail for thirty days for filing a false report. This is all your fault!"

Her logic makes absolutely no sense to me, but then again, it never did. But one part surprises me.

"What do you mean, you don't have a job?"

"Fire marshal came back and shut us down for not taking care of the fire extinguishers and shit. Said it was a public safety issue and we didn't fix it fast enough. Mama argued with him every which way, but it didn't do any good. The Fishbowl is closed until further notice, and that's all your fault too."

I squeeze my eyes shut as a pang goes through me. I shouldn't care because it's part of my past now, but the Fishbowl has played such a big role in my life, so tied up with all my memories of my mama, it hurts to think of it being over.

Where will Earl and Pearl and Jim go? And when did Aunt Laurelyn get back?

And . . . *shit.* What about the ring I hid in the bar? *How am I going to get that back to Boone?*

Shit.

"Hey, I need a drink, if you're still workin', lady." A man waves a twenty in the air next to Brandy.

"Sorry, of course. What can I get you?"

"We're not done here. You can't just brush me off. You owe me. I need money. You should have to pay that fine, not us!" Brandy's voice rises over the din, and the customer backs away from the bar.

Great. Just great.

Hope steps up beside me and crosses her arms over her chest. "She doesn't owe you shit, Brandy, and you ain't getting a dime from her. Now, get the hell out of my bar before I have security drag you out."

"You're a dried-up old cunt, Hope. You two deserve each

other."

Brandy shoves away from the bar and knocks over the drink of the person next to her—on purpose—before disappearing into the crowd.

Hope lays a hand on my shoulder. "You okay?"

My hands tremble, but there's nothing I can do except lie and throw myself back into work. At least if I stay busy, I won't have time to think about any of this.

"I'm totally fine. I got this. What can I get you, sir?" I ask the man who was waving the twenty when he steps back up to the bar.

"Seven and Seven."

"On it."

For the next hour, I lose myself in the mindlessness of serving drinks, making change, and running tabs, blocking out what Brandy said. Even if I wanted to pay the fine, the bar has already taken almost every cent I have.

When the thought enters my brain, I realize I'm going down the same exact path I've always gone—misguided family loyalty. *I don't owe them anymore.* But habits like that can't be broken overnight. Someone else waves a twenty at me, and I get back to work.

When the crowd finally thins around two thirty, I'm dead on my feet.

Hope calls a cab for someone whose liquor has gotten the better of him, and I cover her section of the bar. A man in a cowboy hat sits at the end, his head tilted down.

"Can I get you something, sir?"

The brim of the hat lifts to reveal Boone's piercing blue eyes, and my mouth drops open.

"Seriously?"

He shrugs. "What? You don't like my hat?"

"How long have you been here?"

"Long enough to see your cousin isn't in jail."

Out of habit, I glance down the bar to where Brandy stood earlier. "You saw that?"

"I was about five feet away, ready to intervene, when Hope chased her off. She doesn't get to hassle you. No fucking way."

I meet his familiar blue gaze. "She said they're making her pay a fine, and she might go to jail if she can't. The Fishbowl was closed by the fire marshal indefinitely due to public safety issues."

"She's not getting a single bit of sympathy from me."

"I know. But still . . ."

"Look, finish doing your thing, and we'll talk about this later."

I turn, ready to do what he says because I can't wait to get out of here tonight, but I pause and look back at him.

"You didn't need to babysit me. I talked to Hope. She can give me a ride."

"I said I'd be here, and I'm a man of my word. First thing I'm gonna make sure you understand is that when I say I'm gonna do something, I do it." Boone pauses thoughtfully. "There's a matter of a few orgasms outstanding that I owe you too, and I'll deliver on those as well."

I look both ways down the bar, hoping no one else overheard him.

"You can't say stuff like that to me here." I lower my voice to a whisper-yell. "I'm at work!"

Boone doesn't bother to check the surroundings. He rises from his stool and leans over the bar so our faces are only inches apart. "I don't give a damn who hears me say that I'm taking you home tonight. You're my girl, and it's about time I show you exactly what that means. I'm gonna spoil you, Ripley Fischer. It's about damn time someone did, and I'm privileged to have the opportunity."

My heart slams into my chest, and I have no idea how to respond.

Boone takes advantage of my momentary speechlessness to wrap a hand around the back of my neck and slide his lips along mine.

"Kiss me, sugar. I've missed the taste of you."

Oh God. I've missed the taste of him too. I know I should pull away, but I can't find the strength.

"Good girl," Boone mumbles before his tongue dives inside and there's no talking at all.

I lose myself in the kiss for a few seconds before someone wolf-whistles.

"Get 'er done!"

I jerk back, and Boone releases his hold on me.

"I'll be waiting out back."

There's no question of whether I'm leaving with Boone. That's done and settled. Now, the only question is what happens next.

Do I use this as my chance to say good-bye?

CHAPTER SIXTEEN

BOONE

I open the truck's door for Ripley, then wrap both hands around her waist and lift her into the cab. It's not like she can't do it herself, but I like having my hands on her, and it's been too damn long.

When I climb into the driver's seat and start the engine, Ripley says two words that change my plans.

"Your place."

I look over at her. "You sure?"

She gives me a nod, and I decide that I'm not about to argue with her.

"All right, then."

We don't talk on the drive, each of us lost in our own thoughts, but I come to some conclusions of my own. When the gate slides open, I finally speak.

"This means something to me, Ripley. You mean something to me." I turn my head to meet her gaze as I let the truck roll up the drive and the gate closes behind us. "Give me a chance to prove to you just how good this can be before you give up on us completely."

She thinks I don't know how her brain works, but I'm getting a pretty good grasp on it.

"I can't make you any promises."

I guide the truck into the garage and put it in park before I turn in my seat. "That's fine, but I'm gonna make you one. You will never regret giving us a real shot." Even in the shadows, I can see the hesitation on her face.

"You can't know that."

"Yeah, I can."

Before she tries to argue further with me, I open the door, hop out, and come around to get her. She's already got her door open, but I pull her out of the truck with both arms wrapped around her waist. I carry her inside, never letting her feet touch the floor.

"*You're late*," the parrot shrieks from his cage, but I don't pause to tell him to zip it.

I walk us down the hallway to my bedroom. If I can't get Ripley to believe my words, then I'll prove it to her through my actions.

If I only have one night to convince her not to walk away, I'm going to make the most of it. I'm going to work myself so deep into her soul that she can't move without feeling me.

When I lower her ass to the bed, she reaches for my shirt, but I still her touch, holding her hands together above her head in one of mine while I draw her tank up her stomach.

"You're so goddamned beautiful."

I toss her shirt aside and press a hand to her chest, guiding her onto her back. I take care with her shoes and then her pants, peeling them down her legs, not wanting to jostle her ankle. I drop to my knees and press a kiss to the top of her foot where the bruising still remains.

"But you're also strong and capable. That's sexy as hell. You don't need me, Ripley. I know that for a fact. So I'm gonna make you want me instead."

Something soft passes over her features, and I hope I'm getting through to her.

I spread her legs, taking my time kissing my way up her thighs until I'm an inch away from her center, breathing her in.

"I've never wanted another woman the way I want you. I need you to know that's true. This isn't surface level. It goes deep, all the way to my bones."

My tongue darts out, stealing a taste of her as she inhales sharply.

"You're already wet for me, sugar. Totally soaked. Has this pussy been missing being filled up?"

Sliding both hands under her ass cheeks, I lift her higher against my face, finding her clit and dragging my teeth across it.

"Or have you been dreaming about what it'd be like to have this ass filled?" I press four fingers between her cheeks, finding her back entrance with one and giving it a nudge.

Another harsh breath from Ripley.

"If you don't answer me, I'm going to keep guessing."

"Yes! I missed you. Everywhere. I don't know what you do to me, but . . ."

"But you want more." It isn't a question, because her body is already trembling with need.

"Yes."

I release my hold on her and rise to toe off my boots, tear open my pearl-snap shirt, and shuck off my jeans.

"Then more is what you're gonna get."

CHAPTER SEVENTEEN

RIPLEY

I'm in trouble.

Everything that comes out of Boone's mouth is wearing down my resolve to end this between us before it gets out of hand.

He knows it.

I know it.

And yet I can't stop myself from wanting whatever he's going to give me. He stands before me naked, his blue eyes drilling into mine.

"Right here, right now, it's just you and me. No bullshit. No media. No families. No past. Just us. *This* is what matters. If you can just give us a shot, a real one, this is all that matters. We make the rules. We decide what pieces everyone else gets. We control this, not anyone else."

He makes it sound so easy, even though I know it's not. For tonight, I'm willing to buy into the fantasy he paints. He says I don't need him, but maybe right now, I do.

"Show me," I tell him, and burning heat flares in his gaze.

"That's exactly what I plan to do. Lose the bra."

I push up on my elbows on the bed and reach behind me to unhook it. I've never been a seductress, but with Boone, I wish I were. I let the cups drop forward before slowly drawing the bra away from my skin.

His fingers tense and release with every inch of skin I uncover, like he's fighting back the urge to touch.

Don't fight it. I want your hands on me. I want to forget everything but how you make me feel. My head fills with all the things I can never bring myself to say out loud.

Boone's patience dangles by a thread as I slip the bra off and toss it aside. His voice takes on that gravelly tone in his songs when he speaks.

"Do you have any idea how fucking gorgeous you are?" He drops both palms to the bed and leans forward, capturing one nipple. With a tug, it's hard and aching, shooting darts of sensation to my clit, which is dying for the perfect friction only Boone seems to be able to deliver.

When he finally releases the peak and switches to the other, my breaths are already becoming uneven.

I bury my hands in his hair, holding his head to my chest as I arch up, wanting more. His teeth clamp down on my nipple, nipping and dragging across the sensitive flesh. Heat bursts between my legs, and as much as I love foreplay, I need him to hurry.

Releasing my grip on Boone's hair, I shift so I can reach between our bodies and palm his cock. I can feel his groan against my skin, and my urgency kicks up another notch.

"Please. Hurry."

Boone lifts his head. "What makes you think I'm going to hurry a damn thing? You're meant to be savored, sugar, and all this sweetness is mine."

The heat between my legs is only matched by the burning in my chest when he says things like that.

Don't fall in love with him, Ripley. This is just sex.

I spread my legs and lift my hips to grind against Boone.

"Jesus, fuck. I can feel how damn wet you are." He reaches between us, his finger sliding across my smooth skin. With the tiniest bit of pressure, his finger would slip inside me.

With each spine-arching stroke, Boone plays with me. My hips buck, trying to force his hand, but he pulls back and meets my eyes as he lifts his fingers to his lips and sucks them clean.

"So fucking sweet."

Oh my God. I'm nearing combustion.

"You want my fingers inside you?" he asks.

"Yes, dammit."

"You gonna come for me like that? Squeeze 'em tight and give me more of this sweetness?"

"Yes."

"Maybe you should taste it first. You ever tasted yourself, Ripley?"

My brain stutters. *What did he say?*

But I don't have time to think further because Boone's fingers dip between my legs, thrusting inside, giving me exactly what I want for a moment before drawing back and lifting them to my mouth to paint my lips with my own wet heat.

"Taste."

At this point, I'm not sure if there's any order that could fall from Boone's lips that I wouldn't follow.

I dart out my tongue and lick, but that's not enough for

him. He pushes his fingers between my lips, and the musky, salty-sweet flavor hits.

"So fucking good." Boone draws his fingers from my mouth and sucks them off, and I don't know if I've ever seen anything so dirty yet insanely hot in my entire life. "You like it."

I'm on the verge of telling him I want to know how he tastes when his fingers thrust into me again, this time curving forward to hit my G-spot with each pass. I buck my hips, wanting what's already building.

"That's a good girl. Fuck those fingers. Take them just like you're going to take my cock." Boone palms my hip and squeezes, helping me lift and lower until a silent cry leaves my lips.

Holy hell. The orgasm slams through me harder than ever before, and when my brain starts firing again, I have to wonder if it's the dirty talk that made it even more intense. I've never had someone speak to me like that, and it turned me on more than I ever thought possible.

Apparently, Boone has a silver tongue in more than one respect.

I hold in a giggle as he moves his hand once more, drawing out the remains of the hard-and-fast climax until I finally still. When my breathing loses its ragged edge, his eyes drill into mine.

"Do you trust me?"

That's a hell of a question to ask, and one that threatens to pull me out of this delicious haze. I could analyze it, but I don't want to. For once, I go with my gut, which says there's only one possible answer to that question anyway.

"Yes."

"Good. I'm gonna make you come harder than you ever have before."

I'm about to tell him he's just done that, but Boone grips me by the hips and flips me over before my lips part.

Boone's hand slides between my legs, cupping my pussy. "I'm gonna fuck you hard, the way I've been dying to." With my slickness on his fingers once again, he brings them up to circle the previously untouched territory. "And I'm gonna fill this tight little virgin asshole with my finger."

Is it possible to spontaneously orgasm from just words? I don't know, but I think I just did.

I fist the comforter on the bed, burying my face in it to quiet my moans.

"Let those out. I want to hear 'em. I want to hear every fucking sound you make while I stretch you out to take my cock. Your ass is mine, sugar."

Oh. My. God.

Boone's touch disappears, and the next thing I hear is the sound of him rustling around in the nightstand. When he comes back, a cold drizzle of liquid hits the spot in question.

"Just a little lube."

Before my brain has the chance to form any questions, Boone lifts my hips and strums my clit for a beat before driving inside my pussy, filling me with a single thrust.

I scream out something that sounds like a mishmash of his name and *fuck* and *oh my God*, but the sound is lost to the slapping of his hips against mine as he pounds into me.

"Touch yourself. I want those fingers on your clit. Mine are about to be busy somewhere else."

I do as he says because, duh, I like multiple orgasms, and the combination of pressure on my clit and Boone's cock inside me is a surefire way to achieve them. As soon as I move my hand, he presses against my ass with the pad of what I assume is his thumb, and my nerve endings go wild.

Pressure. Pressure. Pressure.

And then dark, dirty *pleasure*.

"Oh my God. Oh my God." My entire vocabulary has shrunk to this one phrase because I can't seem to recall any other words.

My cries grow louder as he begins to fuck my ass with his finger in time with his thrusts into my pussy.

Soon my whispers turn to keening wails and then screams. My inner muscles clench as I throw my head back and forth. The orgasm barrels down on me, smashing through every obstacle.

"Oh my God!"

Blood thunders in my ears as my entire body convulses. I fall forward, but Boone is relentless. He reaches around and slaps his hand over my clit as he continues to power inside, until I'm a sobbing, shaking mess.

He climaxes with a roar and finally stills.

"Sweet fucking Christ." He presses his lips to my shoulder blade. "You almost gave me a goddamned heart attack."

From the furious hammering against my rib cage, he's not the only one. "Likewise."

"Come on."

"What? No. I can't—"

Boone pulls out of me, no doubt with a mess, but he lifts me into his arms too quickly for me to do anything about it.

Without turning the lights on, he gets us to the shower and flips on the water with one hand. When the steam is billowing, he carries me inside and sets me on my feet. The water washes over me in warm streams, and I don't have to move a muscle because Boone washes my body with a soft cloth, taking care to make sure he doesn't miss an inch.

When he finishes, he speaks into the darkness. "This is happening, Ripley. You and me. I won't give you up."

I press both palms to his hard chest and allow myself to speak the truth. "I'm not ready to give you up either."

Boone whispers something that sounds like *thank God*, and cups my face before taking my lips.

CHAPTER EIGHTEEN

BOONE

I wake to an empty bed.

My first thought is *Fuck, she bolted. I scared her off.* I didn't go easy on her last night, physically or otherwise. But the sheets beside me aren't cold. They still hold the heat of Ripley's body. She hasn't gone far.

I remember the last time I woke up to an empty bed, and what happened next. *I could handle a repeat of donuts and the kitchen table.*

When I roll out from under the covers, my feet hit the floor and I cross to the dresser for a pair of shorts.

My first instinct is wrong, and I find the kitchen empty. Soft singing is coming from the living room, and it draws me forward. Ripley refills Esteban's food tray, but she turns and goes quiet when she hears me behind her.

"I'm guessing that bird's been getting one hell of a show for years now if you sing to him regularly," I say.

"*Superstar,*" Esteban says, and Ripley laughs.

"For the record, he's talking about you, not me." She nods down at the shirt she's wearing, one of my T-shirts that fits her like a dress. "Hope you don't mind that I borrowed it."

"Sugar, you can borrow whatever you need. You don't have to ask." I glance at the clock. "You always get up at the crack of dawn, even after you've worked late?"

She nods. "It's a habit. I used to have to get up and make Pop breakfast, and then I'd go back to bed for a couple hours. I guess I just got into the routine, so now I make myself some breakfast and then sleep until noon. Well, sometimes, anyway."

The thought of how hard she worked for her old man without any thanks makes me want to kick his ass, but that's not going to help me erase the frown on her face.

"Then how about I make you some breakfast this morning, and we go back to bed and work it off."

I'm not sure what I expect from her, but the big grin I get is better than anything I could imagine.

"I think I'll take you up on that."

Two Denver omelets and a double side of bacon for each of us later, Ripley eyes me with new respect. "How did you learn to cook like that?"

"Ma wanted to make sure her sons could look after themselves in the kitchen. I'm pretty sure she didn't want us to fall for the first woman who could keep us fed, because she knows we've got big appetites."

Ripley laughs. "She sounds like an amazing woman."

"She is. Both she and my dad believed in teaching us the value in hard work, so I perfected my omelet-making skills in the kitchen of Country Critter for two summers in high school."

"Country Critter? Sounds . . . interesting. Where exactly did you grow up?"

"East Tennessee. Not too far outside Knoxville. Had the Smoky Mountains in my backyard. God's country." When I think about that view and watching the fog rise off the mountains in the morning, I miss it. I'm due for a trip home.

"Do your folks still live there?" Ripley asks.

"Sure do. In the same house where I grew up. No matter how many times I've tried to buy them a new one, my dad won't hear of it. He says it was good enough for him before, and it'll be good enough until the day they put him in the ground."

Ripley's eyes go wide. "I can guarantee that's not what Pop would've said if I were in your position. He'd be first in line holding out his hand, telling me that I owe him for all the sacrifices he made while I was growing up."

Again, I want to knock her dad's teeth out. It's probably a good thing I've never met the man, because I have a feeling Ripley wouldn't be pleased at the outcome. Instead, I change the subject back to my family, wishing she'd had what I did growing up.

"My brother lives a half mile from my folks. Ma watches his little boy while he and his wife work. They still have Sunday dinner together after church." As I tell Ripley about my family, I realize how much I've missed them lately, and an idea hits me.

"It sounds like . . . it sounds like what you'd see in a movie. Idyllic."

"It's pretty damn perfect. But when I was eighteen, all I wanted to do was go to Nashville and make my mark. I wanted to be famous, tour the world and sing in front of thousands of fans in sold-out shows."

"And you did it." She reaches out and squeezes my arm. "You're pretty incredible too."

I shrug. "I got lucky. Right place, right time, right sound, and the right record exec. That's how it happened, and if any one of those things had been different, I probably would've ended up moving home eventually and working with my dad and brother."

"What did your parents think of you wanting to make it big? Leaving behind the small-town life?"

"They were awesome. Totally supportive. My folks have been to more of my shows than probably anyone else in the world. I owe them everything."

Ripley's hand tightens on my arm again. "They sound wonderful."

An idea keeps rolling around in my head, but it's not ready to be put into words quite yet. Instead, I stand and grab both our plates and take them to the sink to rinse.

"I can do that."

"I'll worry about the dishes. You worry about being naked in bed when I get there."

Ripley's cheeks turn pink. "Are we going to . . ."

The reason for the blush becomes clear. "Not yet. I've still got some work loosening up that sweet little asshole of yours."

The blush darkens, and she spins around and disappears as Esteban squawks, "*Get a room!*"

CHAPTER NINETEEN

O h. My. God. I feel like a broken record because I've said it so many times, but I can't help it. Boone does things to my body I never knew were possible.

Round three in the books, my eyes drift closed. "I'm going to take a quick nap. Only a few minutes."

He presses a kiss to my hair. "Take all the time you need, sugar."

When I open my eyes the next morning, the sun is sneaking through the curtains, and I feel like I've just woken from a coma.

With my arms stretched above my head, I search the room but see no sign of Boone. There aren't any sounds coming from the bathroom either. I grab my jeans from the floor and pull them on, along with another one of Boone's T-shirts. I tie it in a knot at the side so it doesn't hang down to my knees. He's deceptively big. I don't know what it is about him, but you don't realize how massive he is until he's right up on you. The ache between my legs is another sign of what else is massive.

Good God, if all those groupies knew what kind of equipment Boone is packing, he'd be even more overrun than he already is.

A flash of possessiveness streaks through me at the thought of anyone else knowing what I know.

He's not yours, Ripley. Calm down.

Another part of me disputes that because he could be. *All I have to do is say yes.*

I shove those thoughts aside and make my way out of the bedroom to wander the house in search of Boone. The kitchen and living area are empty. I don't see him on the back deck. His truck and his 442 are in the garage, so I know he has to be around somewhere.

Part of me doesn't want to snoop in other places, but when I hear the muffled sound of a guitar drifting up the wide stairs leading into the basement, I follow it.

I make my way down the stairs and realize the basement is just as big as the first floor of the house, which is built into a big hill. Four sets of sliding glass doors run along the back, leading out to a terrace where he set up all the targets for me the other day.

The sound of the guitar grows slightly, but it's still much quieter than I would expect as I make my way down a hall to peer through thick windows.

I finally find the source of the sound.

Holy shit. Boone has his own recording studio.

His back is to me, and the headphones he'd wear if he were recording are hooked on a stand.

This close, I can hear more of the sound coming through the mostly-soundproof walls, and it's like nothing I've ever heard from him before.

He pauses and pulls a pencil from behind his ear. From the hunched set of his shoulders, I assume he's writing lyrics down.

Something akin to awe sweeps over me when it sets in that he's writing a song. Probably something that's going to be played on a million radios and in dozens of stadiums.

Amazing. Seriously amazing. And that thought is followed by, *This could be me someday.*

Is that what I want?

I've barely had time to consider the question and what the consequences would be if I decided to take the leap.

Unlike Boone, I don't have a family to leave behind and miss. What I said about Pop is absolutely true—if I ever made it big, or hell, even made it in a small way—he'd show up with his hand out, expecting to be repaid for everything he ever did for me.

Sadness and grief accompanies the vision playing through my head. *Why couldn't I have a normal family like Boone's? Why did Pop have to drown in that bottle instead of smothering his only daughter with love? Why did someone have to kill my mama?*

I'll never be able to answer any of those questions.

Boone swivels on his stool, guitar in hand, and his head jerks up when he sees me through the window. A smile stretches over his face, and it's like the sun coming out from behind thick clouds to shine its warmth down on me.

When has anyone ever looked at me that way?

Never.

Boone slides off his stool and comes out of the studio. "Hey, Sleeping Beauty."

"You could've woken me."

Boone shifts the guitar out of the way and steps forward to steal a kiss. "Didn't want to. You look like you're owed a few solid nights of sleep. I'm sorry for leaving you to wake up alone. I got hit with a melody that wouldn't quit, so I had to get it down before I lost it."

"Your next number-one hit?" I ask, half joking.

One of Boone's eyebrows goes up. "I guess we'll see."

What would it be like for that to even be a possibility? Do I really want to know?

"I've been doing some thinking, and I want to take you home."

Jerked away from answering either question, I snap my gaze back to Boone with surprise, and a shaft of disappointment surprises me with its intensity. "Oh. Of course. I just need to get my stuff, and I'll be ready. I can have Hope come get me if you're too busy."

A look of confusion crosses Boone's face before it clears. He shakes his head. "No, not your home. Mine. My folks. I want you to meet them. See where I grew up."

I catch my reflection in the glass windows of the recording studio, and I'm not sure my eyebrows could go any higher.

"What? Like . . . soon?" Meeting the parents is kind of a big freaking deal.

One corner of Boone's mouth quirks up. "Yeah, like today."

"*Today*? I can't. I have to work tonight."

"I took care of it."

What did he just say? He couldn't have possibly said what I think he just said.

"Excuse me?"

"I took care of it. I called Hope. She said you can have the weekend off."

I take a deep breath, but my temper gets the best of me. *How dare he?*

"I don't want the weekend off! I need to work. I need the money. That's why I have a job. I can't keep taking time off, because I'll never save any money and get my own place. And weekend shifts are the biggest for tips."

Boone shrugs like it's no big deal. "I'll cover it. You won't lose any money."

My jaw drops open at the fact that he thinks I'd take a handout.

"I'm not taking your money. I *work* for mine, which is why I need to call Hope right now and tell her not to take me off the schedule."

"Too late. She said someone else asked for extra shifts because she's got a sick kid who needs surgery, so she said it worked out perfectly."

He's talking about Lenora, another part-time bartender at the White Horse, a single mom whose baby has been in and out of the hospital since she was born.

I suck in a deep breath, my temper still dangerously close to boiling over. If there's one person I've met who needs money more than I do, it's her. But *still.*

I straighten my shoulders and lift my chin. "Listen. You don't get to run my life or make decisions for me. You don't get to decide whether I do or don't need the cash from working a weekend. You have no idea what it's like to be me, and what it's like to be worried about making enough money so you don't have to eat PB&J for weeks at a time."

The smile on Boone's face fades and his expression goes dark. "You think I don't know what it's like not to know where your next meal is coming from? You think you're the only one who has ever had to worry about making ends meet?"

"You just told me about your perfect parents and perfect childhood and perfect freaking life, so no. I don't think you know what that's like."

Boone's eyebrows dive into slashes between his eyes. "I lived in my car for six months—through the goddamned winter. Some nights I couldn't sleep because my teeth would chatter so hard. If I didn't pull in enough tips at the bar or find odd jobs, I didn't eat the next day. I know what it's like, Ripley, but I also didn't have friends like you do. No one rolled out the welcome mat for me and told me to stay as long as I liked. No one helped me get a job or a break. You're buried so deep in the struggle, you can't see all the good you've got around you."

"Because the struggle is all I know! I can't rely on anyone but me. If I do and it falls through, then I'm even more screwed than I was before."

"You think Hope is going to screw you over?"

"No, but—"

"You think I'm going to screw you over?"

"I don't know—"

"Well, I do. And it's not fucking happening, so just let me help you. I've already given your bird a home for as long as you need it. What else can I do to prove to you that I just want to help?"

"I don't know." This time, instead of sputtering in anger, I whisper it. "I don't know how to do this."

The fear of getting backhanded by life again blazes through me, and Boone curves a hand around my neck and meets my eyes. "Then I'll show you. Give me a chance to prove myself. I'm not him. I'm not any of them."

"You have to promise you're not going to step in and cancel my shifts again. Ever. I've been running my own life for too long to let someone walk in and take over."

"I'm not trying to take over. I just want to give you one weekend where you're not trapped behind a bar. When's the last time you actually did something fun?"

I'm silent for a few beats before I answer. "With you."

Boone finally smiles again. "That was nothing. Just wait until you get the whole Thrasher clan."

CHAPTER TWENTY

My anxiety notches up with each mile that passes. We're in Boone's truck because he wasn't sure how the weather was going to hold out and didn't want to chance it in the 442. I stare out the window with my hands folded in my lap and take in the passing scenery. I've never been to this part of the state, so everything is new.

Actually, I've never been much of anywhere. To Memphis once with Hope so we could see Graceland. I'm knocking on the door to thirty years old, and I've never left the state of Tennessee. What would Boone say if he knew that? He's probably been to almost every state in the union and tons of foreign countries. Places I can only dream about visiting if I stay my course and don't seriously consider what could happen if I tried to make a go of it in the music industry.

"You're awfully quiet," he says.

I look across the cab of the truck and find him studying me. "Just taking in the scenery."

"Nervous?"

To meet his entire family? Is he insane? Obviously, I'm nervous.

"Yep."

"They're good people. You've got nothing to worry about. Ma will love you. I already know that."

"How?" I turn in my seat to face him.

Boone shrugs. "I just do."

"Did she like Amber?" I don't know why I ask the question, but it's out and I can't take it back.

Boone inhales and slowly releases a long breath. "No. She didn't. They saw it way before I did."

This time, I'm studying him as he fixes his eyes on the road in front of us. "Saw what?"

"That Amber didn't want me for me, only for what being with me would do for her. She said all the things I wanted to hear, but I was too blind to see it was all bullshit." He glances at me. "That's why I know Ma will like you. You refuse to take a damn thing from me without being forced, and you don't hesitate to tell me how it is, regardless of what I might think or say."

I huff out a laugh. "You make me sound like an ungrateful bitch."

"No, not at all. More like a proud, independent woman. And considering that's what my ma is, you'll get along just fine."

A hint of relief works its way through my system. I've never done the *meet the parents* thing, but I have to believe his mom is the biggest hurdle. "Tell me about everyone else again."

Boone drops one hand from the steering wheel and

reaches across to thread his fingers through mine before he speaks.

"My dad's a small-engine mechanic. He has his own shop and repairs mowers, lawn tractors, chain saws, generators, basically anything with a small engine. My brother was a mechanic in the service, and when he got out, he went into business with Dad. They've expanded into boats, ATVs, dirt bikes, and stuff like that too. It's a nice business, and they both make a good living. Wendy, my brother's wife, manages a dental office in town. She started out as a hygienist but found she liked being the office manager more than having her hands in people's mouths. She and Grant have a little boy named Kyle. He's five, and cool as shit."

I can't help but smile at the love that's clear from Boone's tone. His family sounds so completely *normal*.

"I've got a dirt bike for him for Christmas that's going to piss Wendy off something fierce, but I know he's going to love it. He already tears it up on the little four-wheeler I got him."

"You bought your five-year-old nephew a dirt bike? Are you serious?"

He nods. "I started riding when I was six. Figured he could have an early start."

"Six? You were riding a dirt bike at *six*?"

"Yeah. We didn't have a lot of money, but Dad had a customer trade him two little dirt bikes to fix a few lawn tractors for his yard-care business. Dad got 'em running, and Ma didn't object. It was my favorite thing to do growing up. My brother and I would head out to the trails and ride for hours."

I could picture a younger Boone doing daredevil stunts on the back of a dirt bike. It's a miracle he's still alive.

"I've got a track out in the back forty at home. I'll teach you when we get back."

"Um, I'm going to take a hard pass."

Boone winks at me. "We'll start you riding the ATV by yourself and work up from there."

I roll my eyes and ask another question. "Is your brother older or younger?"

"Grant's two years older. He joined up when he was eighteen, and when they sent him off to boot camp, I went down to the recruiter's office with a fake ID and tried to sign up too."

"No way."

"Sure did. They tossed my ass out and kept my fake."

"Is that what you wanted to do? Join the service?"

"Dad's a vet. Granddad served. Then when Grant did, it just seemed like I should continue the Thrasher family tradition."

It's not hard to picture Boone in a uniform or camo fatigues. Actually, I probably shouldn't picture him that way because I guarantee he'd look even hotter than he already does.

"Did you try again when you turned eighteen, or were you already dead set on making it in Nashville?"

"This is where I have to say fate stepped in. When I went back on my eighteenth birthday with my real ID, the recruiter took one look at me and knew exactly who I was. He told me he respected the balls it took to try to get in early, but I wasn't cut out for the Army if I wanted to take shortcuts like that. He sent me home."

"For real?" I'm stunned. I figured they'd be thrilled to have him.

"Dead serious."

I know there has to be more to the story, but Boone releases my hand to make a sharp right turn.

"We're almost there. Another couple miles."

Again, the apprehension I felt earlier is back. "What did your mom say when you told her you were coming home?"

Boone slows at a stop sign and looks over at me. "Didn't tell her. Figured I'd surprise her, which is way more fun."

"You didn't tell her?" I ask, my voice going up an octave. I feel like Esteban, repeating part of everything he says.

"Nah. She's been after me to come home, so she's probably partly expecting it."

My anxiety and apprehension kick into overdrive, and Boone must realize I'm silently freaking the hell out.

"Ripley, it's gonna be fine. They'll be excited to see me and thrilled to meet you."

"Why would you assume that?"

Boone turns to me and says simply, "Because you make me happy."

CHAPTER TWENTY-ONE

BOONE

Driving into my hometown with Ripley in the front seat of my truck is a lot different than the first and only time I brought Amber to meet my folks. We were in an Escalade driven by her security, because she didn't think it would look impressive enough if we drove ourselves.

That was Amber, always concerned about how things would look.

Because I wasn't driving on that trip, I caught her every reaction as we drove into town. Amber wrinkled her nose at the Sleeping Giant motel, and made a face like she smelled something bad when she caught sight of the Boot Scoot Honky Tonk.

She asked, "Is this really it?" three times.

I didn't need to see the town through her eyes to know that it wasn't good enough for her, even though she finally stooped to calling it *quaint*.

I turn down my parents' street, wondering how Ripley is going to feel when she realizes that we're going to be sleeping in an apartment over their garage that they fixed up as a guest suite.

Amber had looked around like she was searching for the nearest Hilton. We made it one night before she swore something crawled on her, and then took off with security and the Escalade the next morning. I stayed for the rest of the weekend with my family, getting a ride back to Nashville from my folks, who I treated to a couple of nights in a swanky downtown hotel and tickets to the Grand Ole Opry for their trouble.

My parents are the type who would donate a kidney to one of their kids without batting an eye, so they tried to say no because it was just a simple ride. I wouldn't let them turn it down because I was also trying to make up for the embarrassment Amber caused.

She'd picked at Ma's cooking, asking if she had vegetarian options, even though I'd seen her eat meat before.

It was a train wreck. When I confronted Amber about it a few days later, she gave me some story about being so nervous, and begged me to forgive her. She went on and on about how loving my family was and how sweet they'd been to her, and even though it burned, I let it slide.

I let way too many things slide with her. I was such an idiot. Thankfully, the good Lord was watching out for me, and saved me from making the biggest mistake of my life.

If it were anyone but Ripley, I might second-guess taking a woman home this soon to meet my parents. For some reason, I know she's going to fit in just fine. Maybe my folks will realize my judgment has improved in a big way too, because I'll be proud to introduce Ripley to them. She's an amazing woman.

I'm also hoping that by seeing me with my family, Ripley

will finally start to understand that she and I aren't so different.

Am I using them as my secret weapon? Maybe. But to get Ripley to give me a real shot, I'll do whatever it takes.

"Here we are." I turn down the gravel drive with a white mailbox and a split-rail fence. Just beyond the giant birch tree sits my parents' white farmhouse and barn-sized garage. Ma's mums are in bloom on the porch, and an American flag flies from the pole above the black-and-white POW/MIA flag.

"It's so perfect," Ripley whispers, glancing over at me. "You really grew up here?"

I nod. "Sure did. My parents have lived here for over thirty years."

"Wow." Her tone carries a hint of wonder, reaffirming everything I expected.

The front door flies open and a mutt comes running out, barking his fool head off. I pull up a couple of feet and park behind my dad's truck. It's five thirty on Friday, which means he just got home from work and dinner will be on the table by six.

"They have a dog!"

The excitement in Ripley's voice takes me by surprise. I had no idea she liked dogs.

"They've always had at least one. This is Buford. He's one hundred percent Heinz 57."

When Ripley blinks at me in confusion, I explain. "He's a mutt. Adopted from the pound before they could put him down."

"Can I pet him? I've always wanted a dog, but . . . it wasn't in the cards."

Damn, now I want to give her a whole damn litter of puppies just to see how she'd light up.

"Go on ahead. He's plenty friendly. I'll get your door."

I climb out of the truck, give Buford a rubdown and a pat on the side, and come around to let Ripley out. Once I've got her door open, Ma calls from the front porch.

"It's about time, young man! I'll put a couple extra plates on for dinner." Ma doesn't sound surprised in the least to see me standing in the driveway. She's got a sixth sense about things like this.

"Be right in, Ma!"

The screen smacks against the door frame as she steps back into the house, no doubt to return to the kitchen to make sure whatever she's got cooking doesn't burn.

When Ripley is out of the truck, she hunches over and Buford races full speed, knocking her on her ass before covering her face with sloppy licks. Instead of screeching like a lot of women might, Ripley laughs, sounding genuinely happy.

Looks like I'm gonna be housebreaking a puppy if that's her reaction.

"He's such a good boy!"

When Ripley looks up at me, her eyes shining and her arms around Buford's neck, it hits me. *Game over. I'm done. She's it. The one.*

Now I have to make her fall in love with me.

A few minutes later, gravel crunches in the driveway behind us, signaling another arrival. A truck door slams, stealing Buford's attention away from Ripley. He lets out a long howl and races for the newcomer.

"Baby bro!" my brother calls out. "Ma just called. We've

been waiting to see you in person so we could tell you the good news!"

Ma must have called them when she saw us turn down the damn driveway, not that I'm complaining.

Grant comes around the hood of his truck and helps Wendy down. Her small frame is all belly. She looks like she's about to pop, but I'm pretty sure she's only five months along or so.

I reach out a hand to Ripley and pull her to her feet. She wipes off the seat of her jeans and glances at my brother and his wife as though she's embarrassed to be caught rolling around on the ground with the dog. She doesn't know my family well, because that's probably the quickest way to win them over.

"Who do we have here?" Grant asks, one hand at the small of Wendy's back.

I wrap an arm around Ripley and haul her against my side. "This is Ripley Fischer, my girlfriend." I hear her draw in a quick breath from beside me, but I don't pause. "Rip, this is my brother, Grant, and his wife, Wendy."

"Don't forget me!" The back door to the truck slams and a small body races forward until it collides with my legs. "I had to finish my last level. Sorry, Uncle Boone, I only have five more minutes of game time left for today, and I didn't want to give up until I won. But you're way better than video games. Can we go ride my ATV?"

"Kyle, your uncle Boone was introducing us to his friend. Say hi to Ms. Ripley," his mom says, reminding him of his manners.

Kyle, with his Thrasher blue eyes, stares up at Ripley. "You're pretty. I'm gonna marry a girl as pretty as you someday."

"You trying to steal my girl, Ky?"

His smile is quick and broad, and I drop down to wrap him in a hug. "Missed you, kid. You been good for your mama and daddy?"

Kyle glances back toward his parents before replying. "I kinda caught the yard on fire last week, and Mama yelled a lot."

My gaze cuts to my brother. "What the hell happened?"

"You can't say *hell*, Uncle Boone. You know Lala doesn't like it when you cuss." Lala is what Kyle calls Ma because she's always singing while she's cooking or gardening.

"Thanks for the reminder, buddy." I ruffle his hair, kicking myself for not getting here more often. I'm missing so much of watching him grow up. "Now, are you gonna tell me about the yard?"

Wendy steps forward. "Later. That'll keep." She reaches out a hand to Ripley. "I'm so happy to meet you."

Ripley shakes her hand. "It's nice to meet you too."

Grant is standing back, eyeing Ripley with a healthy dose of skepticism. "Your girlfriend? That's pretty frickin' quick after—"

Wendy steps back and jabs her elbow into Grant's side. "Aren't you going to tell your brother the big news?"

"What news?"

Before Grant can speak, Kyle blurts, "Mama's having *two* babies!"

"Holy sh—shoot. Twins?" I look from my brother to Wendy and back again.

Grant's skeptical look is replaced by a wide grin. "What can I say? It's those Thrasher super swimmers."

"And it explains why I'm as big as a house."

"Oh, wow. That's amazing. Congratulations," Ripley

says. "Do you know if they're boys or girls or one of each yet?"

Wendy shakes her head. "No, we're opting for a surprise this time. All we want is healthy."

"Y'all gonna stand out in the drive all night? Your ma's puttin' dinner on the table in a few minutes."

We all turn to see Dad on the front porch, beer in hand.

"We're comin', Papa!" Kyle takes off at a run, which is pretty much the only speed he moves at these days.

I follow behind him with Ripley beside me.

"You ready for this?" I ask her.

"I hope so."

CHAPTER TWENTY-TWO

RIPLEY

It doesn't take a genius to see that Boone's brother is leery of me. And why shouldn't he be? His kid brother, a superstar, got publicly cheated on and dumped, and then he shows up two weeks later with a new woman in tow?

And then Boone called me his girlfriend and my heart nearly stopped.

We walk up the steps of the white farmhouse that looks like it belongs on an Americana postcard, and Boone's dad stands in the doorway.

"I'm Randall Thrasher. It's nice to meet you."

"Ripley Fischer. I'm sorry we didn't call ahead." I take the hand he offers and shake it.

"No need to call ahead. This is my boy's home. He's welcome anytime, day or night, and so are you. Can I get you a beer?"

"Sure. That'd be great."

Boone shoots me a smile, and I wonder if that was the right answer.

"Ma, we finally made it inside!"

"You think I don't know that? My favorite grandson already found me and told me no one would miss my dinner while it was hot."

Boone's mom steps out of the kitchen. Now that I see her up close, I recognize those same brilliant blue eyes that Boone, Grant, and Kyle all have, although it appears hers have faded some with age. Her hair is a blond chin-length bob, as opposed to Boone's dark hair, which must have come from his dad, although now Mr. Thrasher's is now more salt and pepper.

Stepping inside their house is like walking into the life I wished I could have had as a kid. A cozy couch and love seat situated in front of a fireplace, which has a flat-screen TV mounted over it. I can picture stockings hanging from the mantel at Christmas, with a plate of milk and cookies for Santa nearby, waiting for him to come down the chimney.

The rug is worn, but the flowers depicted on it still hold their color. The tables look like antiques and match the grandfather clock on the other side of the fireplace. The living room opens into a dining room, and the big table is set with enough plates for the whole family—and me.

Mr. Thrasher disappears into the kitchen and returns with three beers for us, and a Sprite that he hands to Wendy with a kiss to her cheek. "You look beautiful, girl. Make sure my boy keeps you smiling like that."

From the way Wendy's lips curve, I'm sure this isn't the first time Mr. Thrasher has said something to that effect.

Kyle comes running out of the kitchen with a red Kool-Aid mustache. "Lala says the veggies aren't done yet. Five more minutes. I'm gonna help finish setting the table."

Mr. Thrasher hands out the bottles to the rest of us and ruffles the boy's hair before Kyle darts off again.

Everything about this house and the people in it screams *family*. Something I haven't had in a really long time, or maybe ever.

"Thank you, sir."

Mr. Thrasher smiles at me as I take a long draw of my beer. "So, Ripley Fischer, tell us about yourself. How'd you meet my son?"

I swallow and fight the urge to bite my lip. I'm sure hearing that I'm a bartender and I met Boone when he came into my bar isn't going to win them over. A worse thought occurs to me. *What if they think I'm some kind of gold digger?*

Boone answers for me. "Ripley's been running her family's bar, and doing a damn good job of it too. I was lucky enough to meet her when Zane Frisco dragged me there one night. I keep forgetting that I need to thank him for that." His arm slips around my waist and his hand squeezes my hip.

Mr. Thrasher's eyebrows go up. "Running a bar can't be an easy business."

"It's definitely a challenge," I reply. "It was in my family for over thirty years, and unfortunately recently closed."

"So, what you're saying is you don't have a job?"

This comes from Boone's brother, and no one in the room can miss the skepticism in his tone. At least I have an answer to my question. He definitely thinks I'm a gold digger.

"I have a job. I'm bartending at the White Horse Saloon while I work out exactly what I'm going to do next. It's been a long time since I've considered the possibility of doing something other than working in a bar. I've been carrying cases of liquor since I was Kyle's age."

Wendy jabs Grant in the side again, and I highly doubt he and I are going to be friends. I can't blame him, though. He's just looking out for his little brother.

"Wow, that sounds like an interesting way to grow up," Wendy says to cover the awkwardness of the moment.

"I had the boys working around the shop when they were growing up too. And let me tell you, Boone here is lucky he survived with all his fingers, for as much as I had to holler at him for messing with stuff."

We're saved from any more awkward small talk when Boone's mom walks out of the kitchen and into the dining room with a steaming casserole dish.

"Come on, y'all. I'm not letting my scalloped potatoes get cold for anyone."

Kyle follows her with a basket covered in a towel and sets it on the table.

"I'll get the ham, Susie-Q." Boone's dad heads for the dining room to set down his beer before disappearing into the kitchen.

"Is there anything we can help with?" I ask Boone.

"Ma would whip my ass if I let you lift a finger this time. You're a guest. You'll have to wait until next time to lend a hand. She's got rules."

"And those rules exempt pregnant women from doing anything more than enjoying her amazing cooking," Wendy says with a smile. "Come on, you're not gonna want to miss this. I swear she sprinkles crack on the food, because no matter how close I follow her recipes, mine never taste as good."

"Come on, baby. You know I said your meat loaf was just

as good as Ma's," Grant says to his wife as he walks into the dining room with us.

"Hush your mouth. You don't want your mama to over-hear that."

"Too late, sweet boy. But you're lucky I love you, or there'd be no more meat loaf for you." Boone's mom strides toward me and wraps me in a hug. "Welcome, Ripley. I'm so sorry I didn't greet you properly earlier. It's like conducting a symphony making sure everything's ready on time. We're so happy to have you in our home. Boone's told me a lot about you, and I've been dying to get a look at you. I knew I was right. He finally picked a good one."

He told his parents about me?

"Ma—" Boone tries to interrupt, but Mrs. Thrasher releases me and hugs him hard.

"Shush your mouth, boy. I'm speaking the truth. We've missed you. We're coming up to Nashville soon. Your daddy promised me a night out on the town, and it's time to pay up."

"Anytime you want, Ma. You know my door is always open, or I'll get you a hotel if you want to stay in town."

"I've told you a million times, I'm fine with staying at the Holiday Inn. It's plenty fancy enough for us."

"Don't you dare stay at the Holiday Inn, Ma. You deserve the best I can give you, since that's what you always gave me."

My heart plops into a big sloppy puddle on the floor.

Boone is a mama's boy, and it's the sweetest thing I've ever seen.

"Sit down and eat. My ham will get cold if I take the time to argue with you about this nonsense."

We sit down at the table, with Mr. Thrasher at the head

and Mrs. Thrasher at the foot near the kitchen. Everyone joins hands as Boone's dad leads us in a prayer.

By the time his mom serves dessert, it's official. I've completely fallen in love with Boone's family.

Well, most of them.

CHAPTER TWENTY-THREE

BOONE

I could wring my brother's neck, just hard enough not to kill him. It's clear he's not sure about Ripley and doesn't like how fast things have moved with us. But that's too damn bad. There's one thing I know about Ripley now—if I give her too much time to think, she'll talk herself out of giving me a shot and I'll lose my chance forever. I'm not about to let that happen.

"Your brother hates me," Ripley says as I close the door to the garage apartment.

"He doesn't hate you." I drop our bags on the bench at the end of the bed.

"If looks could kill, you'd be picking my body bag up off the living room floor."

The very thought of Ripley in a body bag makes my stomach turn, threatening the ham and scalloped potatoes I ate for dinner.

"Don't say that. He's just looking out for me."

"Was he the same way with Amber?" she asks.

I hate to admit it because I know Ripley's going to draw

some sort of conclusion from it, but it's going to be the wrong one. But still, I can't lie.

"He didn't like Amber. He only met her twice, and both times, she didn't give him a whole lot to like. I promise he won't be like that with you. He's in protective-older-brother mode right now. I think it's easy for him to forget I'm thirty-two years old and totally capable of making my own decisions."

"He thinks you're making a mistake with me. That you shouldn't have gotten involved with someone else so quickly. I can't say I disagree with him, Boone. I was supposed to be the rebound, but you didn't follow the rules."

"I'll tell him the same thing I'm about to tell you—it doesn't matter how much time there was between, because it was pretty fucking apparent once I got my head out of my ass that I was dead wrong about Amber. I wanted the line of bullshit she sold me, and I was too fucking blind to realize that's exactly what it was—bullshit."

"What if I can't give you what you want? I don't know how to do this!" Ripley waves toward the house as she keeps going. "You have a perfect family. A mom and dad who love each other and care about you. A brother who would kill someone for you. A sister-in-law who isn't a bitch, and a nephew who's as sweet as can be. They even have the perfect dog!"

"So? What the hell does that matter?"

"You know what I had? A murdered mother who slept around to try to escape her reality of being married to an asshole drunk who didn't have a problem showing her—and me—the back of his hand whenever he felt like it. Oh, and don't forget a lying, freeloading bitch of a cousin, and an aunt I haven't seen in close to twenty years."

"That doesn't mean shit, Ripley. You're loyal and kind, won't accept help unless you're forced, and I'm pretty fucking sure you wouldn't hesitate to throw yourself on a grenade if it meant it would save someone you love."

She goes quiet, and a rough breath leaves her lungs. "But that doesn't mean I know how to be part of something. I know your brother is just looking out for you, but maybe he's right. Maybe you do need more time before you figure out what you want."

I close the gap between us and yank her against me. "I don't need time to know that you're not like any woman I've ever met before, and everything you are is everything I want. Don't try to push me away just because you're scared of what's happening here."

"I'm not scared."

I look her in the eye. "Sugar, you're fucking terrified." I lift a hand to skim along her cheek. "You told me that girls like you don't get a happily-ever-after, and I told you I was going to prove you wrong. I'm a man of my word. I'm done asking you to give me a shot. I'm taking it, because I know I can make you happy. I can give you everything you've been afraid to want. You want front-porch swings and little dark-haired babies, I'm the man who's gonna give them to you. Do you understand me, Ripley? I'm not fucking around. You want a recording contract with a big label and a splashy tour? Then we'll make it happen, and we'll conquer it together. You've never been part of a team before, and it's time you understood what that's like."

"It's too much, too fast. I don't know if I can do this."

"Sugar, all you have to do is try."

CHAPTER TWENTY-FOUR

Boone is slaying me one word at a time. I'm terrified that I'll fall for the picture he's painting and I'll wake up and find out that it's all a dream—or a nightmare. Instead of giving him the answer he wants to hear, I crush my mouth to his.

"You're not gonna distract me," he says on a ragged breath as he pulls away.

"Then consider this me trying."

Boone groans and curses. "Fuck, I want you, but dammit, I've never had sex at my folks' house."

His admission shocks me. "Are you serious?"

"I respected them too much. Besides, I had my truck and that worked fine."

Now I'm trying to picture a younger Boone and what he must have been like. Cocky, arrogant, and probably the hottest guy in school. "You were a total player, weren't you?"

"Now what makes you automatically assume that?"

"How could you not be?"

Boone laughs. "As much as I love your vote of confidence, sugar, I wasn't always a stud."

"Riiiiight, superstar. I don't believe it." I'm sliding back into normal, not-so-freaked-out territory.

"My folks didn't have money. My truck was pieced together from the salvage yard. It was three different colors until I could save up the money to paint it myself in the auto-body class, and I had to carry an extra quart of oil around with me just in case it burned it all. I wasn't anything special. There were plenty of girls that wouldn't look twice at me because I didn't live up to their standards."

"Hey, you got one up on me. I didn't even have a car in high school. And I bet you anything those girls are kicking themselves hard now."

Boone chuckled. "A few of them managed to get meet-and-greet passes and tried to hook up with me after a concert."

"I hope you shut them down hard."

"What do you think?"

"I think you definitely did." My hand skims down his T-shirt to trail over the waistband of his jeans. "Speaking of hard . . ."

"Let's just put this on the table—I know you're distracting me, and we both know you're damn good at it. But this conversation isn't over. We're gonna come back to this, and you're gonna tell me you understand where we're going and you're on board with it."

"There's plenty of time to talk about that later." My voice has taken on a husky tone, and I reach for the button of Boone's fly. "Right now, I'd rather make you come."

With a flick of my wrist, I pop the button and tug down

the zipper. He groans when my hand closes around his cock.

"So, are we gonna go for a ride in your truck, or are you finally going to man up and bang a girl at your parents' house?" I can't help but giggle as I say it. "Although, you should know, I'm not opposed to the truck . . ."

"Oh, I'll definitely have you in my truck one of these days. Don't you doubt it for a second. But tonight . . . tonight we're not leaving this room. I swear, you're the only one who could tempt me into this. You're dangerous, woman."

I squeeze him a little tighter.

"You're only saying that because my hand is wrapped around your dick."

Boone catches my hand and squeezes it tighter. "Nah. You won't break me, sugar. Feel free to get a little rough."

An impulse slams into me, surprising me enough to have me stumbling over my next move.

I want him in my mouth. I want to drive him so crazy he can't remember his own name. I want him never to forget this night or me.

I'm not the kind of girl who gets to her knees for a man, but with Boone . . . something's different.

Maybe it's the fact that he's never asked me. Never even brought it up. Or maybe it's because he's gone down on me multiple times, never expecting anything in return.

Whatever it is, I want this. I slide to my knees, ready to break a long-term ban on giving head, but Boone grabs me by the elbows and hauls me up.

"I don't want you on your knees. I want that pussy on my face."

Heat pulses between my legs. "Okay."

"Attagirl."

He kicks off his jeans before stripping off mine and tipping us both backward onto the bed. I land on top of him.

"First, give me this mouth. I can never get enough of this mouth."

"I was trying to—"

"Shush."

His lips capture mine, and I lose myself in the kiss. His tongue sweeps inside, tasting and teasing, before his teeth nip my lips and I nip back.

"You'll always bite back, won't you?"

"I give as good as I get."

Boone's blue eyes blaze. "Guess we're going to find out right now." He sits up. "Spin around and give me that sweet pussy."

Oh God. Sixty-nine? I've never been a fan of that . . . but then again, with Boone, everything is different. I guess I don't have to worry about putting my ass in his face since he's already laid claim to it. *I'm going for it.*

With a smirk and zero shame, I shift into place, my legs spread over Boone's face, and he wastes no time gripping my ass and pulling me closer. I've barely got my lips to the head of his cock when he devours me.

It's everything I can do to keep my focus on the goal. And I completely and utterly *fail.*

Two orgasms later, both mine, I finally scoot down Boone's body.

"This is so not fair," I protest.

"What? That you can't help but lose your mind when my lips touch your pussy? Not sure why you sound upset about that."

"Because this was my show. My turn."

He shakes his head and grips his cock with one hand. "Then by all means, sugar. Climb on and take it home."

Being on top is another thing I've never really loved because of the way everything bounces and jiggles, especially if it's not pitch dark in the room.

Boone notices my hesitation. "You change your mind?"

It's time to woman up, which isn't exactly a hardship with the way Boone is staring at me.

"Things jiggle when I'm on top," I confess.

Boone's eyebrows go up. "And thank fuck for that. Do you have any idea how sexy you are when those sweet tits are bouncing? God, I'm halfway ready to come just thinking about it. And being able to get my mouth on them while you ride me . . . shit. I'm gonna have to fight to make it last. And when I get my hands on that luscious ass of yours . . ." He groans. "I'm a goner. Hell, I'm already a goner, Ripley. You've got me. The only thing you're gonna do is pull me in deeper by dropping that guard and tossing those inhibitions aside. Can you do that?"

When he puts it like that . . . "Yeah, I can."

I situate myself on top of Boone and do exactly that.

CHAPTER TWENTY-FIVE

BOONE

W hen I decided to make the impromptu trip home with Ripley, I totally forgot the rodeo was Saturday night. It closes the season and is a big event for the town, which means the Thrasher family always shows up in full force.

"You ever been to the rodeo, Ripley?" Ma asks as we walk toward the gates at the edge of the fairgrounds.

"No, ma'am. I haven't. I've always wanted to go, though."

"You're in for a treat. But get ready, everyone will want to see Boone."

"Shouldn't you have security with you here?" Ripley asks me quietly, concern in her voice.

"Nah. Not here. If someone tried to pull some shit, the entire town would be on them in a heartbeat. This is probably the safest place I could be, other than at home."

"Are you sure?"

I think it's sweet that she's so worried about me. "Sugar, despite what you think, I can handle myself if something goes down."

"If you say so." The disbelief in her tone makes me want to prove it to her, but I'm beyond the stage in my life where I go looking for a fight.

"Boone's a hometown hero," my dad says. "He's done so much for this place, they've even dedicated the new baseball stadium to him. Thrasher Field has a great ring to it."

"Seriously?"

I don't usually talk about all the charitable stuff I do, because that's not why I do it.

"I was home one weekend, and Kyle and I decided to swing by the field and catch a tournament game. The old baseball diamond where I used to play was a wreck. The bleachers were empty because people were terrified they were going to collapse. It wasn't right, so I offered to help."

There's a different light in Ripley's eyes when she looks up at me. "That's really cool of you. So you don't just rescue women with sprained ankles and take them to the hospital against their will? You're quite the do-gooder despite your bad-boy reputation."

Ma cranes her head to get a better look at me when she hears what Ripley says, and I swear I see approval on her face. "He's as good as it gets, Ripley, and I'm not saying that just because he's my son."

After we pay for our tickets, we spot Grant and Wendy waving from the grandstands where they've saved us seats with a couple of plaid blankets. Usually it's Ma and Dad who do the seat saving, because Grant and Wendy are late more often than not since Kyle was born five years ago, but they managed to pull it together tonight.

"There's Arlene and Arty Johanson. Rand, we gotta go say hello so I can ask about their new grandbaby. She was over the moon to finally have a first."

Dad knows how Ma is about keeping a finger on the pulse of what's happening in town, so he just says, "Lead the way, Susie-Q."

She glances at me. "We'll be back in a few."

"Take your time, Ma."

The crowd thickens as we near the grandstands, and I reach down and curl my hand around Ripley's, in part to keep her close, but also because I like it. When we reach the foot of the stairs that will take us up to our seats, a voice stops me.

"Well, I'll be damned. Look who lowered himself to come home and mingle with the common folk."

Ripley's head turns sharply in the direction of the drawl coming from inside the metal stock fence that separates the rodeo action from the crowd.

"I thought you just got yourself dumped, Boone? You already moved on to greener pastures? Must be nice being such a hotshot that the ladies can't keep their hands off you."

I squeeze Ripley's hand before releasing it in favor of draping an arm around her shoulder and turning to face the skinny man in jean shorts five sizes too big held up by hot-pink suspenders. The uniform of a rodeo clown, and the description fits him perfectly. Lou Biggler never quite forgave me for that one night his sister sneaked her way into my truck and I politely told her to get out. He tried to beat the hell out of me in phys ed the Monday after, but I gave him a black eye instead and we both got suspended.

"Hey, Lou. Thanks for saying hi. Good to see you."

I attempt the polite route, even though I'd rather tell him to fuck off. But he's the type who'd sell any dirt to the papers for a dollar.

"How long's this one gonna last? I swear, you had a record with the last one, but it turned out she was a little too smart for you since she decided to jump ship."

I don't acknowledge his comments. Instead, I put to work the gossip Ma still feels the need to share with me regularly. "I hear you're on divorce number three, Lou. Hope that's goin' smoothly. Good luck with the custody battle this time around. Maybe four will be your lucky number."

Lou's clown-painted face twists into a harsh smirk. "You just love to come back to this town and act like King Shit, but we all know you're nothing special. Anyone could sing into a microphone and let those computers fix their voice. I hear they do it all the time. Shit, it's harder to stand in front of the damn bulls that'll be coming out tonight. If you had a real pair of balls, maybe you'd be out here instead of me."

"Nah, Lou. You got big enough balls for both of us. Makes sense why you gotta wear the extra-large shorts to cover those massive nuts."

He reaches down and grabs his crotch, apparently uncaring that there are little kids present. "They're just keeping up with the size of my massive—"

"Louis Biggler, you better not be about to say what I think you're gonna say." Ma's voice cuts through the crowd before I can respond. "Because I know a father like yourself would never use any kind of foul language around children."

Lou straightens up real quick, dropping his hold on his dick. "No, ma'am. We're just catchin' up for old times' sake. Didn't mean no harm."

"That's what I thought. You be careful out there tonight. We need to make sure you get home in one piece to those little angels of yours."

"Yes, ma'am. Will do, ma'am."

Ma turns to Ripley and me. "Let's get our seats, shall we?"

She leads the way up to the third row where Grant and Wendy and Kyle are seated, and I throw a last glance back at Lou. His eyes are narrowed on me like he hasn't forgotten a damn thing, and his chin lifts when he sees my look. Some people never lose the chip on their shoulder.

When we slide down the row to take our seats on the blanket Grant laid out, he gets up to run Kyle to the bathroom. Wendy says she has to pee too, and my parents offer to get drinks and popcorn for everyone.

"That guy was interesting," Ripley mutters once we're alone.

I press a kiss to her temple like it's the most natural thing in the world. "That's small-town life for you right there. He's been harboring a grudge since our junior year of high school."

"Sounded to me like he's jealous."

I shrug. "Maybe. A lot of these people still remember me as a punk kid who drove a loud truck too fast and took out a few of their mailboxes, or maybe believed a rumor that I got their daughter or sister or cousin in the backseat. That's where it ends for them. Then they see me on TV and can't figure out how that punk kid got so damn lucky to be living the good life. Doesn't seem fair, I expect."

Ripley's brows draw together. "Do they not realize that you paid your dues to climb to the top? Or how hard you bust your ass to stay where you are? Or what you sacrifice to be away from your family? Or what it's like to have the paparazzi threatening to capture any moment of your life you think might be private? If they don't see all that, they're only getting a fraction of the picture."

Hearing Ripley leap to my defense so quickly and with such ferocity tells me that I'm making progress. It also turns me way the fuck on. I shift to face her and lift her chin before stealing a kiss.

"It sounds like you might actually like me," I murmur against her lips.

"Shut up. You know I like you."

I pull back a fraction of an inch and meet those stormy gray eyes. "I'm wearing you down. Pretty soon, you're gonna fall in love with me."

CHAPTER TWENTY-SIX

RIPLEY

Boone's words crash into my chest, and instead of causing a heart attack, they kick off a cascade of warmth that envelops me. This time, I'm the one who leans in and presses our lips together.

"Get a room, Thrasher!"

The call comes from below us, and I jerk back and look around. "Shit. I'm sorry. I wasn't thinking. Crap. There could be pictures—" I'm ready to curl up with embarrassment when Boone lays his hand on my thigh and squeezes.

"Let 'em watch. You're my girl, and I don't give a damn who knows it. Especially not this asshole."

A big man approximately the size of a grizzly bear shakes the bleachers as he stomps up the three steps toward us.

"Damn, brother. It's been a coon's age!"

Boone stands and does this backslapping man-hug thing with the guy, and I'm worried that the giant might knock him down. Boone's over six feet tall, and yet this guy looks like he's around six eight with shoulders that are massive.

"Jerry Lee, you're gonna break my damn back one of these days."

"Nah, you can take it, tough guy. You didn't tell me you were coming back to town. I just heard the gossip running through the crowd all the way up at the announcer booth." He finally glances over at me. "You're a sweet little thing, aren't you? Boone, how you always finding the most beautiful women to take around? Do I need to sell a million damn records before I finally find a winner?"

Boone laughs his ass off. "No, man. You just gotta quit hanging out at the lodge with all the old men."

I hold out my hand. "I'm Ripley."

"Damn, even your name is super cool. I swear, this joker gets all the luck. You another country star, sweetness? Those lips and eyes could sell me a record without even hearing your voice."

"Hey now, reel it in. I'm not letting you put the moves on my girl right in front of me."

From his tone, I can tell Boone is joking, but also that his buddy likes the idea that he could put the moves on me, and Boone does it to puff up his ego. I've seen plenty of male posturing and weird behavior in the bar, so this isn't exactly new territory for me.

"I'm a bartender," I say. "I don't know about a record, but I could sell the crap out of some Jack and Coke."

"Shit, I guess I need to start spending a lot more time in bars."

Boone sits down and slides his arm around me again. "You ain't gonna find another woman like her. Guaranteed. So, what's going on, Jer? You came all the way down from the announcer stand to try and steal my girl? Because I'm not letting you snake this one like you did Cindy Hooper."

"You're never gonna let me live that down, are you?"

"Hell no."

Jerry Lee shrugs and looks at me. "Cindy Hooper was the head cheerleader, and Boone here thought he had her in the bag. Turns out, he counted on that one too quick."

"Asshole."

"Ha, like you care. You've obviously upgraded, and Cindy's married to a garbage man in Chattahoochee. I think things turned out for the best. Besides, that's not why I came down here. When I heard you were in town and visiting our fine little rodeo, I knew I had to ask you to do the honors."

"What honors?" I ask.

"Sing the national anthem, of course." He looks at Boone expectantly. "What do you say, man? Give the town a show?"

"I'm not here to attract attention, Jer. I wanted Rip to meet my folks and have a fun weekend."

"You're about as good at laying low as I am at gettin' dates. Look around, everyone's already talking 'bout y'all. Might as well give 'em a show."

Boone looks to me. "You mind?"

"Me? No, of course not." I'm shocked he'd even ask, and then I remember he was used to being with Amber Fleet. One guess says she was a diva who didn't like having him take the spotlight off her. "Go do your thing. Give them all something to talk about in church tomorrow. Besides, you can show that asshole Lou that you don't need Auto-Tune." I shoot him a wink.

A smile stretches over Boone's face. "You're so goddamn perfect, it's almost scary."

"So that's a yes?" Jerry Lee asks.

"That's a yes."

"Hot damn! This'll get the rodeo on the front page for sure now. We've been trying to beat out the garden club's annual election, and this seals it. Come on down with me, and I'll get you set up."

Boone stands up and looks around. His parents, brother, sister-in-law, and nephew are all still gone. I can read the hesitation on his face.

"Go. It's fine. I'm a big girl."

"They'll be back in a few."

"I'll hold down the fort. Go give 'em a show, superstar."

Boone leans down and wraps a hand around my neck before pressing a hard kiss to my lips. "I'll be back soon."

He follows Jerry Lee down the bleachers, and I'm left alone with the blankets.

"Well, I'll be damned. I never thought I'd see the day when Boone Thrasher finally found himself a keeper."

I turn around to see an older woman, probably about Boone's mom's age, with her arms crossed and an aluminum Budweiser bottle hanging from between her fingertips.

"Excuse me?"

"Trudy Miles. Boone's unofficial godmother. But damned if that boy was gonna notice me tonight when he doesn't have eyes for anyone but you. And you don't seem to have nearly as big a stick up your ass like the last one."

"Trudy, you keep your tongue in your head." Boone's mom stops beside me, her arms full of three bags of popcorn. "Where the heck did that boy get off to, leaving you all alone?"

"He went to sing the national anthem, ma'am."

"She even calls you *ma'am*, Susie. How precious. You

better tell that boy to keep this one. She doesn't seem like a bitch."

I'm officially in the twilight zone, caught between two ladies who clearly have a lot of history, and I'm fresh out of words.

"As long as Boone likes her, we're happy for him." It's not exactly a ringing endorsement from Mrs. Thrasher.

She takes a seat, and Boone's dad comes up the steps with four Bud Lights.

"Where the hell did Boone go?"

"National anthem," his mom says, repeating the answer I gave her.

"Really? I'm surprised. He didn't want to last time."

"Well, we all know why that was."

It has to be because of Amber. I want to ask, but it's not my place.

Mr. Thrasher hands me a Bud Light. "Knew that girl was a diva from the minute they pulled up, and she screamed and practically climbed Boone to get away from Buford."

"Oh, shush. She's in the past and we can all be happy about it, but we don't need to bring her up every five minutes. We don't want to make Ripley uncomfortable."

"It's fine," I say. "I know this whole thing must seem a little fast—"

Of course, Boone's brother chooses that moment to return to his seat with his wife and son in tow.

"You think? He's barely been single for five minutes before he shows up with you. He's always rushed into shit. Remember when he used his fake ID at the Army recruiter's office?"

Boone's dad speaks up. "I rushed your ma. Proposed on

the second date. Took me until the fifth to get her to say yes. Ain't nothing wrong with going after what you want."

"Still, I think he needs some time to sort his shit out."

I don't know what possesses me to add my two cents to a conversation that clearly doesn't need my input, but I do anyway. "Boone seems to know his own mind."

Grant's skeptical gaze skewers me. "If he does, then you certainly won the jackpot in the lottery of life. He better get a damn prenup."

Even though I should expect it, the venom in his words catches me off guard. "Are you serious? You think I'm trying to hook up with him for his *money*?" I try to keep my voice down, but the accusation makes my tone grow shrill.

"You had a job when you hooked up with him, and now you don't. I feel like that's no accident," Grant says.

Boone's brother is kind of a dick.

"Because he decided to have an impromptu show in my bar, it got shut down by the fire marshal for overcapacity, and then I got my ass reamed and ended up losing the job I've had since before I was old enough to legally work. My entire future was tied up with the Fishbowl, and after your brother's help one night, I ended up homeless and unemployed."

Grant's brows dive into deep slashes. "What the hell are you talking about?"

"You want more? I took a job working for a friend who let me sleep on her futon. I was back at work behind another bar as fast as I could get there so I could earn some money, because I sank my entire savings into keeping my family business afloat. So don't tell me I'm looking to Boone for a handout. I was pissed that he arranged for me to get this weekend off because the tips are better on Friday and

Saturday, and I'm missing out on a chance to hopefully save up for a deposit on my own place."

Mrs. Thrasher tilts her head and shakes a finger at her son. "Grant, what have I told you a million times? You know better than to judge."

He crosses his arms. "Let's just say after that last one left him hanging when he was gonna propose, I'm a little protective of my brother."

"Good. That's great. But I'm not a damn thing like her. I've worked my ass off, and even though I don't have jack crap to show for it right now, I will someday." I infuse all my determination in my words.

"I like her," Boone's dad says before he takes a swig of beer. "She's feisty. She'll keep Boone on his toes and stop him from getting too impressed with himself."

Mrs. Thrasher opens her mouth to say something else, but the announcer's deep voice booms through the speakers.

"You all ready for a rodeo tonight?"

The crowd cheers in response.

"Then let's get this show started! We've got a special guest here to kick us off with the national anthem. Please stand, remove your hats, and face the flag at the north end of the arena. Here's Nashville recording artist and home-town hero, Boone Thrasher, to sing it for y'all."

Boone walks into the arena from the direction of the chutes, microphone in hand, and that deep gravelly voice silences the crowd.

With my hand over my heart, I face the flag, but my eyes are glued to Boone. The national anthem isn't exactly the easiest song to sing, but he *kills* it. Shivers run down my spine as he belts it out. The entire crowd cheers as he reaches the end, and then start chanting his name. "Boone! Boone! Boone!"

Boone turns and waves to the crowd as the rodeo clowns come running out, ready to entertain the masses.

Then all hell breaks loose.

CHAPTER TWENTY-SEVEN

BOONE

I hear it before I see it. The clang of metal against metal as they load a bull into the chute, and the slamming of a solid ton of weight against the gate.

I whip around to see the gate fly off as the hinges fail. Then my eyes zero in on the pissed-off bull's horns and the snot dripping from its nose as its hooves thunder toward me.

Lou is closer to the bull, his back to it as he faces me. I don't know if he's been momentarily struck deaf, but he doesn't turn around.

"Lou!" When I yell his name, he looks at me instead of the bull.

Fuck. It's gonna run him right over.

Hesitation could mean his skull being crushed in the dirt, so I don't think. I bolt toward him, throwing myself at him like I used to in football practice. I swear I see the whites of the bull's eyes before my body connects with Lou's, shoving him out of the way.

The animal turns and bucks, spinning toward us.

Something hard cracks against my head before everything goes black.

CHAPTER
TWENTY-EIGHT

RIPLEY

It's like one of those *Caught on Video* shows where you know something horrible is going to happen. You don't want to watch, but you can't take your eyes off the screen.

A bull charges from the chute as the rodeo clowns come out, and people start screaming. The guy in his hot-pink suspenders from earlier doesn't turn. Doesn't look. Doesn't see the massive beast charging at him.

But Boone sees it.

"Please, God, no!" Mrs. Thrasher's hand is over her mouth.

Everything happens so fast, I barely have time to comprehend what I'm seeing.

Boone dives at the man and the bull changes direction, its hooves flying, and one catches Boone in the head. He goes down, landing limply on top of the man who was such an asshole to him when we arrived.

I don't even think about moving. Next thing I know, I'm out of my seat and running down the bleacher stairs, then throwing myself over the fence. I land on my hands and knees in the dirt and scramble up to take off in a sprint. The other rodeo cowboys and two men on horses are rounding up the bull and corralling it toward the pen, but all I see is Boone's unmoving body on the ground.

People scream, sirens wail, but my mind goes blank when I see the blood dripping down the side of his face.

Red. The same color as the puddle on the bathroom floor around my mama.

No. I can't lose him too.

"Boone!"

I'm terrified to touch him. Terrified to move him, in case he has some sort of head or neck injury. My limited first aid knowledge comes back to me, and I rip off my long-sleeved shirt and hold it to his head to stop the bleeding.

"Ma'am, you have to move. You can't be in here." Someone touches my shoulder, but I slap them away with the other hand.

"What the fuck happened?" The body beneath Boone's shifts, and Boone's head lolls to the side.

"Don't fucking move, asshole. Stay right there." My voice snaps out with the order.

"Paramedics are coming. Ambulance was already here in case of an emergency."

Someone else drops to his knees beside me in the dirt. "Fuck. Fuck. Fuck!" Even from our limited acquaintance, I recognize the voice. It's Boone's brother. "Hold on, little brother. You're gonna be just fine. Wake up, Boone. Come on, man."

The paramedics run into the arena with a backboard but I don't move the shirt, now soaked with blood, from Boone's head.

"Ma'am, we need you to move so the paramedics can help. They're gonna take good care of him. I promise."

My body is frozen in place, the blood staining my hands.

"Ripley, come on, we gotta let them help." Grant lays his hand over mine, breaking me loose from my paralysis.

I jerk my gaze away from Boone to meet blue eyes so much like his. "I . . . He—"

Grant wraps both arms around me and pulls me to my feet as the paramedics drop the backboard and get to work.

"I know. I know. He's gonna be okay. He's got a hard head. He's a tough son of a bitch. They don't grow 'em any stronger than the Thrashers. I promise you. Let's get over to the ambulance."

My hands shake as all the discordant thoughts crash together in my head. My eyes stay fixed on Boone as Grant drags me away. Tears stream down my face as they move him off Lou and start to work on him.

"He's gonna be fine. I swear." Grant repeats the words over and over as he walks us toward the gate where the ambulance is waiting.

A crowd rushes the fence, all eyes on Boone.

"Ma!"

Mr. and Mrs. Thrasher shove their way through the people to get to the gate.

"Is he—"

"Unconscious. Who's going in the ambulance?"

"I'm going to get my truck. Grant, give me your keys," Mr. Thrasher says, and Grant throws his keys to him. "I'll give them to Wendy so she can take Ky home and wait for us to call."

"One of you give this girl a shirt," Mrs. Thrasher says,

staring down at my tank top. I didn't even notice the chill bumps prickling my arms.

"It's okay. I'm fine." My focus is on the backboard they're carrying toward us.

"Someone's gotta go with him. Ma?"

My heart twists at the thought of letting Boone out of my sight for a single second.

"Ripley? You want to go?"

Boone's mom's voice catches me off guard, and I tear my gaze away from him to look at her.

I shake my head. "You go, ma'am. I don't know his blood type or if he's allergic to any drugs. They'll need the best information they can get, and as much as I want to crawl in there beside him and not take my eyes off him, he needs you more."

Something passes over her face, but it's gone before I can identify it. She gives me a nod. "We'll see you at the hospital. My boy is tough. He's gonna be just fine. You'll see."

"I know. He has to be. There's no other option."

Mrs. Thrasher rushes away from us to the open doors of the ambulance and climbs in.

Grant wraps an arm around me. "Let's go. Dad'll pick us up at the entrance."

With Grant at my side, we push through the crowd, not giving a damn that people are trying to talk to us and ask us what's going on. Hell, we don't even take an extra second to be polite. We're likeminded in one single purpose—to get to the truck and then to Boone.

Mr. Thrasher's truck is idling at the gate, and Grant pulls me around to the passenger side and yanks open the door. "Get in."

I climb up and he hops into the backseat. Once the doors

are closed, Mr. Thrasher takes off, steering around the people in the parking lot.

"Bet you can beat 'em there, Dad."

"We'll get there at the same time. I ain't taking chances with either of you two."

Tense silence chokes up the cab of the truck until Grant finally breaks it.

"Fuck, I'm going to have to apologize to him if this is anything like he felt while I was being airlifted to Germany."

I remember Boone saying he was on a USO tour when his brother was injured in Afghanistan.

"That was the hand of God making sure my boy wasn't alone in his time of need."

"Where was the hand of God tonight with the hoof of that fucking bull?"

Mr. Thrasher shakes his head. "Doesn't matter as long as he's okay, and he's gonna be okay."

When we pull up in front of the hospital fifteen minutes later, Grant and I both jump out of the truck like it's on fire. The ambulance is already parked at the doors to the ER, so we rush inside. Boone's mom is standing in the waiting room, her arms wrapped around herself.

"They took him back to be examined. Told me to wait out here for a few minutes." She looks at me. "Grant, give Ripley your sweatshirt. Poor thing is freezing."

I'm shivering, but it's not because of the cold. "It's fine. I'm okay." I look down at my hands, streaked with dried blood from Boone's head, just like they'd been covered with blood from my mama.

I have to get it off. I have to get it off.

I jerk my head around, looking for the sign to the restroom. When I see it, I look at Grant and Mrs.

Thrasher. "I'll be right back. If they come out . . . please . . ."

Grant glances down at my bloodstained hands and then meets my eyes. He nods at me like he gets it. "We'll wait for you."

"Thank you," I whisper before making a beeline toward the ladies' room door.

No one else is inside the institutional white bathroom, and I'm thankful for the privacy. I pump soap from the dispenser and flip on the water, scrubbing my hands together harder than necessary, but *I have to get it off.*

I look into the mirror as I rinse, my eyes wild.

I could lose him. In the flash of a moment, the possibility slaps me in the face again. I haven't even decided if I want to make this real, and I could already lose him. A tear breaks free and tracks down my face. I drop my gaze. I can't watch myself cry because I'll end up bawling like a baby, curled into the corner, and Boone deserves better than that.

That thought doesn't stop another tear from sliding down or the vise that binds my chest, crushing it and stealing my breath. *I can't lose him. His family can't lose him.*

The tears come faster now, and the blood still hasn't come off my hands. I get more soap from the dispenser and keep scrubbing to try to take my mind off the path where it was headed, but I can't.

My reflection is impossible to make out now with the tears clouding my vision, so I blink and look up at the ceiling.

That sweet little boy can't lose his uncle. Please, God, if you're out there listening, please don't put this family through the hell of losing him. I know they're strong, but they're good people, and they don't deserve this.

Before I can start making promises about what I'll do if he'll just let him live, someone pushes the door open and walks toward the stalls.

I duck my head and attempt to wipe my tears on my bare shoulder. After I rinse my hands one more time, they're finally free of blood. I grab paper towels from the dispenser and use them to erase the tear streaks on my face as well.

It's not until I'm leaving the bathroom that a thought crosses my mind.

What would I have been willing to promise to make sure Boone pulls through?

When I see his family huddled in the corner of the waiting room, his dad curving an arm around his mom's shoulder and Grant squeezing her hand on the other side, I know the answer.

Anything.

They look like such a solid unit that I don't want to cross the floor to interrupt them. I'm an outsider, and I know it. I fold my arms around my now chilling skin and squeeze.

Grant releases his mom's hand when he spots me and rises to his feet. He strides toward me and yanks off his hoodie before stopping in front of me and draping it around my shoulders.

"You're not gonna say no. I could see you shivering from across the room."

Cocooned in the huge sweatshirt, I push my arms into the sleeves and curl my fists into the fabric.

"Thank you. I would've been fine."

"Maybe so. But Boone would kick my ass, and Ma would ask what happened to the manners she beat into me as a kid, so we'll just go with it."

"Thank you," I whisper again.

Then he shocks me. Grant closes both arms around me and squeezes me against his body.

"It's gonna be okay, Ripley. He's stubborn. He's got too much life ahead of him to do anything but live it on his own terms."

The tears that were falling fast in the bathroom spill over again, and sobs rack my body. "You can't lose him. Ky needs an uncle. Your mom and dad—"

Grant hugs me tighter. "We're not gonna lose him. None of us are. You included." He presses a kiss to my head and holds me for long minutes as I cry my tears on his shoulder.

No one held me when I cried for my mama. I curled up by myself and sat in the corner of the bathroom after I mopped the floor, bawling until I had nothing left, so I appreciate this hug more than Grant will ever realize.

I've known Boone's family for just over twenty-four hours, and they've already given me more than mine has in almost thirty years. That thought sends another wave of tears spilling over.

Finally, I snuffle back my sobs, lift my head, and swipe at my eyes. "Thank you for that."

Grant meets my gaze, and instead of the skepticism that was there only a couple of hours ago, I now see approval.

"I'm the one who should thank you."

Before I can ask him what he would possibly need to thank me for, he adds, "Come on. Let's go sit with Ma and Dad. We're stronger when we lean on each other."

His simple words hit me deep inside.

We're stronger when we lean on each other. I've never had that. I never thought I would have that. And now, in this family's nightmare, the guy who I thought was an asshole is drawing me into the fold.

"Okay."

We cross to the corner of the room where Mr. and Mrs. Thrasher wait, and sit in silence until a man in scrubs comes out from behind double doors and turns toward us.

"You're here with Mr. Thrasher?"

"Yes. We're his family," Mrs. Thrasher responds, and the description causes my heart to clench.

"He's awake, but we're taking him right now for a CT scan to check for further damage. We'll get you back there as soon as he's done. Please have a seat, and I'll be out shortly."

He's awake!

"Praise the Lord," Mrs. Thrasher whispers, grabbing my hand and squeezing.

Mr. Thrasher crushes her to his side. "Thank God. You know we raised a strong boy."

I thought I was all out of tears, but when more cascade down my cheeks, Grant pulls me against him and pats my hair.

"I told you it's gonna be just fine, Ripley. He's tough. Hard head."

I hiccup, wanting to say something, but the words escape me.

Mr. Thrasher gets up. "I gotta do something. I can't just sit here."

"Go get us some coffee. It's gonna be a long night, so I'm thinking we can use it."

"Sure thing, Susie-Q. I can do that." Mr. Thrasher strides off toward a hallway.

I pull away from Grant's shoulder and swipe at my eyes. "I'm so sorry. I don't usually cry—"

He gives me a soft smile. "It's okay."

"Grant, call Wendy and give her the update. Have her tell Ky that Uncle Boone is okay. He was freaking out something fierce," Mrs. Thrasher says.

Grant gives me a nod and stands. "Will do. That boy loves his uncle." He walks toward the doors to step outside and make his call, leaving Mrs. Thrasher and me alone in the corner of the waiting room.

The matriarch of the Thrasher clan doesn't screw around when it comes to family, and I respect her for that.

She reaches over and clutches my hand again. "You looked like a warrior princess running to her fallen man on the battlefield. That's what Rand said. He's always had a more fanciful imagination than me, but I have to say he's right in this instance. That bull wasn't even contained when you threw yourself over the fence, girl. What the hell were you thinking?"

I meet her faded blue gaze and blink back more tears that burn my eyes at the rough emotion in her voice.

"I didn't think. I just . . . I had to get to him."

"Any woman who'd put herself in the path of two thousand pounds of bull to get to my boy deserves my respect, and you have it. I'll never forget that moment for as long as I live." She pauses. "One thing you can always count on—love makes us do stupid things."

Her last words shock me.

Love?

She studies my face carefully. "You don't even realize it, do you?"

"I'm . . . He . . . I . . ." My stammer comes out sounding ridiculous.

Mrs. Thrasher squeezes my hand again. "It's okay, Ripley. You'll figure it out soon enough for yourself. But I'll tell you there's not a single soul in that arena tonight who has any doubt about how much you care for my son. You didn't have to say a word because everyone saw it in your actions."

Care. Okay, I can handle that. "Of course I care about him. He's a good man. Maybe the best one I've ever known."

Her grip on my hand tightens. "And the fact that you only see the man and not the star tells me that you're as different from the last one as you could possibly be."

It feels wrong to bring thoughts of Amber into this waiting room, but I can't say I'm not curious when Boone's mom tells me I'm different.

"What do you mean?"

"That girl wouldn't have lifted a finger tonight. She might've wrung her hands and worried about how this would affect her, but there's no way in hell she would've climbed a fence in her stilettos and run through the dirt to get to his side, let alone ripped her shirt off and used it to staunch the bleeding. I might be an old lady from the country, but I got a knack for reading people. You were closed up tighter than a drum when you first walked into my house. Not letting any of us see the real Ripley or how you felt about my boy. I decided to give you the benefit of the doubt because Boone told me plenty that gave me hope. When I met you, I wasn't totally sure, though." She pauses meaningfully. "But I'm sure now. He finally picked a woman worthy of him, and I don't say that lightly."

The doors to the ER open and close as Grant paces in front of them, talking on the phone.

"I see your true colors, Ripley Fischer. You may not realize you're in love with Boone yet, but I see it. Just as clearly as I see that he's in love with you."

Grant hangs up and crosses toward us in time to catch the tail end of what his mom says. My stomach knots, wondering what he's going to say.

He tucks the phone away in his pocket, his gaze moving from me to his mom and back.

"She's right, you know. I thought you were gonna be like Amber, fake and clinging to your lottery ticket, but you're a different breed. I mean that in the best way possible."

Mr. Thrasher returns with four cups of coffee in a cardboard carrier. "Kid in the cafeteria says that the news crews are already showing up. Don't know who tipped them off, but they're here. You see 'em out there, Grant?"

Grant nods. "Yeah, a couple of guys."

Mr. Thrasher hands out the coffee. "Anything else I miss?"

We all know he's talking about the doctors and Boone, so my jaw drops when Grant answers him. "Ma and I are about to lay bets on how long it takes Ripley to become an official part of the family."

Mr. Thrasher offers a giant cup of coffee to me. "Not long, if that boy's as smart as I think he is."

CHAPTER TWENTY-NINE

BOONE

My head feels like it's been trampled by a herd of cows instead of just one pissed-off bull, but once the doctor staples the gash shut and they run me through a bunch of tests, they decide I'm not gonna kick the bucket anytime soon.

"We'd like you to stay overnight for observation as a precaution."

I look at the doctor and ask him point blank, "If I wasn't me, but instead was some poor schmuck with no insurance, would you have me staying overnight?"

"Well, Mr. Thrasher, this is a different situation—"

"I'm taking that as a no."

"Boy, if they want to keep you overnight, you stay overnight." Ma's voice comes from the private room's door as it creaks open.

"Ma, I'm fine. I just need someone to wake me every couple hours to make sure the concussion doesn't kick my ass."

"Sir, it would be best if you—"

"I took a hoof to the skull, not a bullet. I'll be fine, Doc. Get my discharge rolling. I'll sign out against medical advice if I have to. Doesn't matter to me." My gaze slides past Ma to clamp on Ripley. "I want to get out of here before the vultures descend."

"Too late. They're already here," Ma says.

I shake my head but realize quickly that's a mistake when it pounds harder. "Of course they are. All the more reason to get the hell out."

"I'll take care of those papers for you, Mr. Thrasher."

"Thanks, Doc."

Ripley doesn't speak until the door closes behind the doctor, leaving her and Ma inside.

"Are you crazy? If they want you to stay, you should stay." Ripley crosses her arms over her chest, and I give her a sidelong look.

"This coming from the woman who didn't want to step foot in the hospital, even though I thought your ankle might be broken? You're not the only stubborn one here."

"No, but she might be the bravest. You should've seen her throw herself over that fence. I wonder if anyone recorded it," Grant says as he walks in.

I look at Ripley, but her gaze darts away. It sounds like there's a story there I need to hear.

Grant pulls out his phone and starts searching. "Sure enough, here it is."

Ripley's face turns bright red. "Are you serious? Who would film that? Why weren't they calling 911? What is wrong with people?"

"Give it here." I hold out my hand.

"Boone, it's not important. You need to rest."

I want to see that video even more than I want to close

my eyes and give in to sleep. I grab the phone from Grant and ignore the pounding in my head.

The angle must have been from someone higher up in the grandstand because they don't catch Ripley until she hits the stock fence and flings herself over. She lands in the dirt, then sprints toward me and skids to her knees. My heart clenches when I see the bull still running free for a good thirty seconds before they have him contained.

My gaze cuts from the phone to her dirty jeans and then back to the screen. I watch the rest of the recording and see how Grant practically had to drag her away from my side.

When I hand the phone back to him, there's a fist gripping my heart and squeezing. I see it, and from the looks on my parents' and brother's faces, they see it too.

Ripley's in love with me.

From her expression, she's goddamned terrified. One more reason I need to get out of this hospital.

The nurse knocks and opens the door. "All right, Mr. Thrasher, I've got your paperwork."

"Good. I'm ready to get the hell out of here."

Grant goes out to get his truck, and we plan to meet him at a side entrance where the press hopefully won't be waiting.

Ripley and Ma walk on either side of the wheelchair the nurse insisted I ride in. I was going to argue, but it wasn't worth it. Besides, I'm still a little woozy, and I'm not giving anyone a reason to say I should stay in the hospital a minute longer.

When we get to the door, Grant's truck is idling, and there's not a skulking paparazzi in sight.

"They didn't follow me, but who knows how long that will last," he says as he hops out of the truck to open the door for me.

"Can't a guy get kicked in the head without the world knowing about it?" I ask, trying to inject some lightness into the moment.

"Not when it's you, superstar," Ripley says, taking my lead.

Grant guffaws at her nickname for me, and they all watch as I concentrate on putting one foot in front of the other and not shaking as I climb up into the backseat of the truck. Ripley rushes around and gets in the other door, then slides over to the middle.

"You should've stayed overnight. Your face is white as a sheet, and if you tell me you feel okay, I'll know you're lying."

The fact that she can read me so easily is actually comforting.

"I'm gonna be just fine, sugar."

Her hands clench into fists on her lap, and I reach over and cover one.

"But—"

"Ripley, look at me." I wait for her eyes to lift. "It'll take a hell of a lot more than a ton of bull to keep me from being with you." Her eyes shimmer in the glow of the fading dome light. "But if you ever put yourself in danger like that again, I swear to God, I'll make sure you can't sit for a week for being so stupid."

Her mouth drops open. "Stupid? Are you serious—"

"Fuck, yes. I'm serious. Next time you let the professionals handle it, and you stay on the sidelines where you're safe. If anything happened to you . . ." I trail off as Dad opens the front door of the truck for Ma.

She twists in the seat and looks back at us. "I think we've had enough excitement for one night. I'm ready to go home."

"Sounds like a plan, Ma."

CHAPTER
THIRTY

RIPLEY

I don't sleep. The clock ticks over past midnight, one, two, three, and I sit up, watching Boone's chest to make sure he's still breathing.

I tried to get him to sleep in the main house with his folks, but he refused. *Stubborn ass*. Buford followed us up to the apartment and curled up on the floor next to the bed, keeping us both company and offering Boone comfort.

Every couple of hours, I wake him up just like the nurse instructed. Each time, my stomach twists until he opens his eyes and smiles at me.

The last time, he finally tells me, "I'm not leaving this earth yet, sugar. You haven't told me you love me yet."

"Then I'll never tell you, because I refuse to let you ever leave."

Boone falls back asleep with a groggy smile, and I assume he won't remember a thing about it in the morning.

When seven o'clock rolls around, I'm fading, the effects of the hospital coffee long gone. Boone sits up in bed just as I'm drifting off.

I bolt upright, my head swiveling around. "What's wrong? Are you okay? Do you need me to—"

One thickly muscled arm wraps around me and pulls me against his hard chest.

"I'm fine. It's okay. Calm down, sugar." He presses a kiss to my hair and holds me close.

With my ear to his chest, I listen to the strong, even beat of his heart and take comfort in every thump. "I'm so fucking glad you're okay." His arm loosens when I speak, and I look up at him. "Don't scare me like that again. I'm not sure I can handle it."

His blue eyes stare down at me with an expression I can't quite identify. "I think you've already handled more than most people will in a lifetime." His voice goes quiet. "But that doesn't mean I'm going to let you get away with not saying you love me."

My eyebrows shoot up. "You remember."

Boone nods slowly. "Of course I remember. I don't forget anything about you, and especially not something like that."

My heart hammers now, so hard that I'm afraid tachycardia might be imminent.

"I was trying to get you to sleep. It was just—"

"Shhh. You can hold it in for as long as you need. I'll be waiting, sugar."

His gaze is soft, and I can read in it all the things he's not saying.

He's falling in love with me.

I swallow back the lump in my throat, trying to control my rioting emotions.

Boone's stomach sends up a loud, perfectly-timed growl, and Buford hops to his feet and lays his chin on the bed.

Boone and I both reach out to pet him, and our hands collide.

"I bet you'd tell me if I got you a puppy."

"Don't you dare. I already have a foul-mouthed parrot living at your house."

"We'll see."

I roll out of bed, ready to change the subject. "We need to get you fed."

"Shower first," he says, stretching his arms above his head with a yawn.

"You have to be careful with the staples."

"Then I guess you're going to have to help me," Boone says with a wink, looking way too incredibly attractive for someone who got kicked in the head by a bull not even twelve hours ago.

"All right, superstar. Sponge bath, it is."

I didn't actually give Boone a sponge bath, but I did help him make sure he followed the care instructions for his head wound.

When we make our way to the house, the scent of bacon and sugary sweetness hits my nose.

"Ma must've gone all out, because that smells like her homemade sticky buns and bacon."

The deep timbre of Boone's voice carries through the house, and Mrs. Thrasher sticks her head out of the kitchen. The smile that sweeps over her features is enough to light up the whole house.

"Thank the Lord." She comes toward us, and Boone wraps her in a hug.

"Sorry to scare you, Ma."

"You've been scaring the life out of me since you were five years old and climbed onto the roof of the barn because Grant said you could fly."

"Oh my God, he didn't . . ." I'm picturing a Kyle-sized Boone on the roof, and it's enough to give me a heart attack.

"He only broke one leg. The two mattresses they'd stolen off their beds cushioned most of the fall."

Oh my God.

"That's what happens when you have boys," Boone says, like it's no big deal that he could have died at five.

Boone's mom looks to me. "You better hope you have girls. Boone will keep them wrapped up in cotton batting and never let them out of his sight."

Boone's arm comes around me, and I wonder if he can feel the tense set of my shoulders.

"Now you're scaring Ripley, Ma. I haven't even gotten her to admit she's my girlfriend, so if you skip right to babies, you might send her running for the hills."

Mrs. Thrasher shoots me a wink. "I think she's made of stronger stuff than that. Come on, I've been keeping the sticky buns warm in the oven for you, and I suppose if you give me a hug, I'll share my bacon too."

Four hours later, Boone has finally proven to his family that he's okay.

"Ripley and I have to head back to Nashville so she can work tomorrow, and I've got a couple interviews I shouldn't miss."

"Interviews? Are they going to make you famous?" Kyle asks.

Boone laughs, and Wendy ruffles Kyle's hair. "Your uncle Boone is already famous, kiddo."

"No, he's not. He plays catch with me in the yard. Famous people don't do that."

Good point, little man. A smile tugs at my lips. Boone is definitely not your average celebrity. Seeing him here with his parents and nephew, I have a whole new outlook on who he really is.

Which is exactly what he probably planned. Diabolical man.

"Are you coming back for Thanksgiving and Christmas, Uncle Boone?"

"You know I wouldn't miss them for the world. But I might have to work, so they could be short trips."

"If you don't come, I'm gonna eat all of Lala's mashed potatoes."

Boone swings Kyle up into his arms. "I can't let that happen. Looks like I'll be here for sure, just to make sure I get some."

He squeezes the little boy to his chest before setting him down and crouching in front of Wendy's belly.

"Listen up, little guys or girls or little guy and little girl. You stay cookin' as long as you need. We'll be ready to meet you when you decide you're ready."

"Now you're talking to them like you talked to Ky?"

"Of course. They gotta know their uncle Boone's voice when they come out. That way when I hold them at the hospital, they'll fall asleep like little angels in my arms."

Wendy rolls her eyes, but it takes everything I have to keep my ovaries intact. Since when did I think it was drop-dead sexy for a man to like babies?

Oh, right, since forever. Me and every woman in the history of ever.

Kyle throws his arms around my waist while I'm still recovering from my mental picture of Boone holding a newborn. I hug him back and ruffle his hair.

When Kyle releases me, he turns back to Boone. "Make sure to bring Ms. Ripley too. I like her. She's pretty, and she smells nice too."

Boone comes toward me, wrapping an arm around my shoulders and bringing me against his side in what has become a regular move of his.

"Damn right, I'll bring her back. You've got good taste, kid."

Kyle throws himself at me one more time, and I give him another hard squeeze.

"It was good to meet you, buddy."

He bounces from me to Boone once more, and I can't keep the smile off my face. The grip I've been keeping on my heart slips another notch at the thought of so easily sliding into their family.

"You make sure you let Ripley drive. I don't care how much you love that truck, it's doctor's orders." Boone's dad steps into the living room after refusing my help to load our suitcases in the truck.

"Dad, I'm fine."

Mr. Thrasher crosses to me and picks up my hand before dropping the keys in it and closing my fingers around them. "Ripley's driving."

A chuckle works its way out of my throat. "Don't worry. I won't scratch her."

"Be safe, both of you." This comes from Boone's mom.

"Yes, ma'am. I'll make sure he calls you when we get back to Nashville."

"Thank you for taking such good care of my boy, Ripley." She comes toward me and wraps me in a hug. "You're always welcome here. Always."

The burn of emotion works its way up the back of my throat and tingles behind my eyes.

"Thank you, ma'am. I appreciate that."

Mrs. Thrasher pulls back and meets my eyes. "He won't break your heart. I taught him better than that," she whispers before releasing me.

Buford meets us at the truck, and I drop to my knees to snuggle him one last time. "I'm gonna miss you too."

"Probably not as much as he's going to miss you." Boone gives the dog a good long scratch behind the ears before holding out a hand to me.

Buford gives my face a lick, and I kiss his silky head before letting Boone haul me to my feet.

"Don't worry, you'll be seeing him again. I promised Ky I'd bring you back, and I'm a man of my word," Boone says as he opens the driver's door of his truck.

Do I dare believe him? What his mom said echoes through my head. *"He won't break your heart."*

I guess we'll find out.

CHAPTER THIRTY-ONE

BOONE

One of the security guys waves at us as we drive through the gate, and I remember it's Sunday and Anthony's day off.

He better have made sure Esteban got breakfast.

Ripley shifts the truck into park once she brings it to a stop in the garage. "Is it weird that this is actually one of the better birthdays I've had?"

My gaze cuts in her direction.

"What did you say?" The words come out a lot harsher than I intended, but that fits with the level of my shock.

"I said it's one of the better birthdays—"

"Why the hell didn't you tell me it's your birthday?"

Ripley shrugs. "I don't know. It wasn't a big deal. It never is."

I look up at the headliner, asking the Lord to send me down some patience so I don't shake this woman.

"How am I supposed to do something special for you if you don't frigging tell me it's your birthday?"

Ripley's expression wrinkles with confusion. "You don't need to do anything special. It's just another day."

"That's where you're wrong." I pull out my phone and start barking orders when Anthony answers the phone. *Sorry about your day off, man.*

When I hang up, Ripley puts her hand on my arm. "Hey, whoa. That wasn't necessary. I've had twenty-nine other birthdays that were no big deal."

I lock my eyes on her stormy gray ones. "Wait. It's your *thirtieth* birthday?"

She nods. "Yeah, but that still doesn't make it a big deal."

"Jesus Christ, woman. Some notice would have been appreciated so I could make it a damn good one."

"It already was. I spent it with you." The words come out so matter-of-factly, and then her lips clamp together as though she realizes what she said.

That's right, Ripley. You feel something for me, and it's not a little something. It's big and scary, but it's real.

The simplicity of her statement stabs me through the chest. This is what it's supposed to be like.

She's mine, and she's staying mine. She might not realize it yet or know how to put it into words, but what I saw on that video at the rodeo is the truth—Ripley's falling in love with me.

"I think we can make it a little better."

I lean toward her, and she presses a hand to my chest. "You need to take it easy, superstar. I want to see your ass on the couch, kicked back and watching TV. I'll get you a soda and find something to make for dinner."

"Anthony's bringing takeout and a cake."

She rolls her eyes. "Not necessary."

"Completely necessary. Now, let's go inside where you can exercise your birthday-girl privileges and pick what you want to watch while we wait."

She picked *Boondock Saints*. If there was any remaining question of whether Ripley was the perfect woman for me, that ended the discussion. I was ready to watch whatever chick flick or rom-com she wanted, but Ripley again proved that she's not like anyone else.

Mine.

The garage door opens and Anthony calls, "Honey, I'm home, and I brought dinner."

"*Shit house.*" Esteban has been an asshole during the entire movie, repeating lines and phrases. Apparently, he's expanding his vocabulary.

Anthony walks into the living room and glances toward the cage. "Did that damn bird just call me a shit house?"

Ripley tries to stifle her laugh but fails. "I think he means brick shithouse, if it makes you feel any better. I'd say that's as close to a compliment as he gets."

Anthony shakes his head as he stares in the bird's direction. "Guess he gets a pass."

Anthony is built like a brick shithouse, and I'm trying to recall if I've said that in front of the bird or if his creative streak is stronger than I realized.

"How many words and phrases does he know?" I ask Ripley.

She shrugs. "I googled it once and read they can learn over two hundred, but he's still shy of a hundred."

"Smart cookie."

We all look toward the bird as he preens. Then I take in the bags in Anthony's hands.

"You get it all?"

He nods. "Obviously. Girl, next time, it would go a long way if you could give me some advance warning for this shit. I know I'm pretty damn amazing, but miracles take a little more time."

Ripley's cheeks turn pink. "I didn't need a miracle. I didn't need anything."

Anthony crosses over to the table and sets the bags down before fishing something out of one.

"Not true. You definitely needed this." He comes toward us with his hand tucked behind his back. When he stops next to the couch, he reveals a silver tiara with pink rhinestones.

Ripley's eyes go wide as she looks up at Anthony, at the tiara, and then to me. "You didn't need to do that," she whispers.

"Every woman needs to be a princess sometimes. Happy birthday," Anthony says, settling it on her head.

"Damn, man. If I didn't know better, I'd think you were trying to snake my girl."

Anthony winks at me. "Just forcing you to raise the bar. If you'll give me another minute, I'll set out dinner and put the cake on the counter for when you're ready. Shit, I forgot the balloons in the car. Hold on."

He disappears, and Ripley adjusts her tiara and shakes her head at me.

"What?"

"You."

"What about me?"

"You're something else."

"A good something, I hope."

She smiles and her whole face lights up. "The best."

I decide in that moment I'd move heaven and earth to bring that smile to Ripley's face as often as possible.

CHAPTER THIRTY-TWO

RIPLEY

Boone turns off the lights and walks toward the table with candles glowing atop the cake. As he walks, he sings "Happy Birthday" in the most devastating rendition I've ever heard.

When he stops, I'm dangerously close to tears. I rein it in and take a deep breath, preparing to blow out the candles.

"Hold up. You gotta make a wish first."

The top of the cake looks like it's in danger of setting off the fire alarms with all thirty of the candles, so I know I need to think fast if I'm going to have any frosting that's wax-free.

"I don't need anything. This is already perfect."

"Just make a wish, Ripley. Something big and scary that you've never dared wish before."

With his face flickering in the candlelight, something comes to mind. Like Boone ordered, it's big and scary, and I've never let myself think about it before.

"That. That right there. Whatever you're thinking right

now, hold it in your mind and blow out those candles, birthday girl."

I swallow back the lump in my throat and take a deep breath. Part of me is terrified to do it because of what it could mean if that wish came true, but another part of me jumps to the forefront and makes sure every flame is doused by the time I finish.

"Happy birthday, Ripley," Boone whispers before his lips slide across mine, stealing a kiss.

When he pulls back, my mind is blank except for the wish shining like a beacon.

"I need two vodka tonics with lime, a Budweiser, and a margarita," one of the cocktail waitresses calls across the bar, and I snap into action.

It's Tuesday, and one of Nashville's hottest new artists is setting up onstage. The White Horse is packed tonight. Hope is off, and the rest of us are hustling to keep up with orders from people at the bar and waitresses on the floor.

I set the drinks on the tray and slap the ticket beside them.

"Thanks, hon." With a nod, the waitress disappears into the crowd, balancing the tray like the pro she is.

I give my ankle a stretch, still feeling the twinge that creeps up on me. Running down the bleachers, vaulting over a fence, and sprinting through dirt at the rodeo didn't help matters, but I'd do it all again in a heartbeat.

I move down the bar, wiping it with a rag as I go, and look up at the next group to take their orders. I freeze as I make eye contact with the two women.

Holy. Shit.

I look around, but no one seems to notice that a country music legend is sitting at the bar, or that one of the hottest female artists of the year is perched on the stool next to her.

Tana Vines and Holly Wix.

Actually, now I suppose she's technically Holly Wix Karas, wife of the infamous billionaire who tracked her down after a one-night stand and married her. I followed the whole story on a gossip site that I now avoid after seeing pictures of me with Boone on there.

Pull it together, Rip.

"What can I get for you, ladies?"

"Sprite for me," Holly Wix says with a smile. "But Tana needs a glass of your best red."

Tana shoots Holly a look. "You told me you were planning on pumping and dumping. You can drink, dammit. I'm not drinking by myself."

"I can't do that. It just doesn't feel right."

Tana rolls her eyes. "Wait until kid number two. You won't think twice about it."

"Either way, I'm not drinking tonight. We're lucky Crey was still in his office, or I probably wouldn't have made it out of the house in the first place."

My gaze bounces back and forth between them like a Ping-Pong game.

"That man . . . I swear. He would've put a team of ten security guys on us rather than just my two."

For the first time, I see the two men in suits taking up space just to the side and behind the women, blocking them from view with shoulders the size of linebackers.

"That's why we have to make this quick before he tracks us down, swoops in, and carries me out of here."

My eyebrows shoot up. I knew this Karas guy sounded like an asshole in the press, but . . .

"You know you love that alpha shit. God knows I do too. When Mick lays down the law and says he's going to paddle my ass . . ." Tana shifts. "Anyhoo, there go my panties."

I feel like I'm overhearing a conversation I shouldn't be privy to, but I can't stop listening as I fill a glass with ice and Sprite and reach for our best bottle of red.

I set the glasses in front of them, and it hits me that Holly and Boone have recorded duets together. They even did one live . . . Oh hell, was that the night Amber stood him up? *Crap, it was.*

Her presence here can't be a coincidence.

"Is there anything else I can do for you, ladies?"

Holly leans an elbow on the bar and looks me in the eye. "Yes, there's one big thing. I'd really like to hear you sing, Ripley Fischer. Someone showed me a video, and I couldn't believe what I was hearing. And then I saw another video, and I called up Zane Frisco to get the scoop."

Shock has stolen my vocabulary, but that doesn't seem to bother Holly because she keeps speaking.

"Frisco filled me in on all the gossip I've been missing while living in mommyland, which included the fact that I was really talking to the wrong person, so I gave another old friend a call."

"Boone?" I guess.

Holly nods with a brilliant smile on her face. "And my dear friend Boone mentioned that you were thinking about talking to some labels, so I had to rip him a new one because the only label you should be talking to is *mine*. I'd like to hear you for myself first, but I think it's safe to say that Homegrown Records is very interested in you."

Oh. My. God. *Holly Wix's label is interested in me.* Holy. Crap.

"Did Boone put you up to this?"

Tana interrupts. "Oh, honey, no. I got to hear one side of that call, and Holly was dragging information out of that boy one piece at a time. She's been talking about you nonstop for three days. I mean, you may have sealed the deal when you threw yourself over a fence to save him from a stampede, but this is as real as it gets. Boone doesn't have a clue we're here."

"It was one bull."

Tana waves me off. "Pfft, I won't even go near a cow unless it's grilled and on my plate, so you're Xena: Warrior Princess in my book."

Holly's gaze turns shrewd as she studies me. "She's right. Once I realized you were a badass bitch *and* had a set of pipes, I knew we had to talk, and soon."

"Hey, can I get a drink over here?" a man yells from a few feet away.

"Don't you holler at her. She's busy!" Tana's thick drawl attracts more attention than she realizes.

"Holy crap, you look just like Tana Vines."

"Impersonator, honey. If I didn't, I'd be pretty shitty at my job."

"What do you need, sir?" I ask the man.

"Four Buds. Bottles, not draft."

I look to Holly and Tana. "I'll be right back."

I hurry to the cooler and pop the tops off the bottles and serve them up.

"What about me?"

With an apologetic glance at the two women, I serve four more customers. When I finally make my way back to

Holly and Tana, it's to find two men heading toward them, parting the crowd in the bar like the Red Sea.

"Oh shit," Tana says.

Holly takes a sip of her Sprite. "Double shit. They both found us."

The infamous billionaire Creighton Karas is just as forbidding in person as the media has made him out to be. His dark hair and expensive suit scream *don't piss me off because I'll bury you.* His gaze is fixed on Holly, and I could swear the rest of the people in the bar don't even exist to him.

"Tana, what the hell are you doing?" The voice belongs to another country legend—Mick Vines, Tana's husband. In their day, they caused their own media firestorm.

Behind both men trail two more guys in suits.

"Hey, baby," Tana drawls. "I'm almost ready."

"Holly." Karas's tone is quiet but firm.

"Yes, my love?"

His hard features go soft for a moment. "Is there something I'm missing here, because your text said you had a late meeting that was urgent."

"I did. We're almost done. Crey, meet Ripley. She's Homegrown's hottest new prospect."

His gaze shifts to me, and with the intensity of his stare, I wouldn't be surprised if he has superpowers that enable him to see down to the depths of my soul.

Karas's chin lifts. "The pleasure is all mine, Ms. Fischer."

His statement doesn't require a response, for which I'm thankful because I don't know what the hell to say to this imposing man. Then it slaps into me.

Wait, how does he know my last name?

There's only one explanation I come up with. This guy is *scary*.

"Babe, let's go. Paps are already circling." This comes from Mick.

"Those assholes are worse than turkey buzzards." Tana downs the rest of her wine. "I guess I'm ready, but we didn't get a firm answer out of Ripley. Holly needs to hear her sing so she can sign her to the label."

"That may be the case, but unfortunately, it's not happening tonight." Karas delivers the verdict.

Holly rolls her eyes. "Then I guess I have to come back tomorrow for open-mic night so I can hear what I need." She looks to me. "Does that work for you, Ripley?"

"Holly—"

"Shh, Crey. We'll have more security. It'll be fine."

He pinches the bridge of his nose. "Damn right we will." His attention zeros in on me one more time. "Make sure to let management know that my security team will be contacting them in the morning to go over plans."

"Uh, okay?"

"Crey, if you scare her, she's not going to want to sign with Homegrown. Boone already told me I had my work cut out for me to convince her, so I don't need you making it more difficult."

"He did?" I ask.

Holly winks. "He told me quite a bit, and I'm so happy for you both." Her smile disappears. "As long as you don't screw him over like that bitch Amber, we'll be all good. Otherwise, you should know that I know people in *the family*."

The family? Holy shit, is she talking about the mob?

"And on that note, I think we're done here," Creighton Karas says with finality in his tone.

"'Bye, Ripley!" Holly and Tana both wave as they slide off their stools. "See you tomorrow!"

I watch as the entire contingent makes its way out of the White Horse, half the crowd standing gape jawed and the other half snapping pictures like crazy.

What the hell did I just agree to?

Boone has a lot of explaining to do.

CHAPTER THIRTY-THREE

BOONE

Holly's practically bouncing in her seat, and her excitement is contagious.

Seeing Ripley on video is a lot different from seeing her perform live. Even though I've got all the confidence in the world in her, I'm still a little nervous. Shit, I'm more nervous than before I step onstage in front of thousands.

Tonight's attendance has been heavily curtailed due to Creighton Karas's ironhanded rule over security, but I can't blame the bastard. When Holly told me she showed up here last night with only Tana and two guys, I asked her if she'd lost her damned mind. She flipped me off. I miss that girl. After touring with her, she became like a little sister to me, and I'm glad as hell to see her succeeding and finding her own happiness.

When we talked last night, she also broke the truth to me about the fact that she never liked Amber. She thought Amber was a bitch from day one, and was irate that she'd fucked me over, but happy I'd parted ways with her.

Hindsight being twenty-twenty and all that, I couldn't disagree with Holly. I also wanted to shake her and ask her why she hadn't bothered to tell me in the first place. But then again, no one did. Not my parents, my brother, or my friends. No one. They just let me almost make the biggest mistake of my life—a mistake that meant I never would have met Ripley.

That thought is enough to twist my gut into knots.

"What's she singing tonight?" Tana asks from the other side of the table.

"I don't know. She didn't tell me."

I don't mention that Ripley was too pissed off at me when she called because I had the keys to a rental car delivered . . . and it was parked in the spot where her Javelin was before Anthony stole it. Although it wasn't really stealing. He just got a wrecker to put it on a flatbed so we could take it out of state.

Regardless, she was fucking pissed.

"She killed that Carrie song. I'd love to hear her sing something else, though," Holly says.

"I guess we'll find out."

"Next up, we've got the White Horse's own Ripley Fischer!" the announcer calls, and Ripley climbs onto the stage with a guitar in hand and wearing her White Horse tank and tight black jeans with tall black boots.

Fuck. She looks gorgeous.

Behind us, the crowd yells, and Holly and Tana both cheer.

Ripley walks straight to the mic and doesn't make eye contact with anyone. She doesn't introduce herself or speak to the crowd before she puts the guitar strap over her shoulder and starts with a few chords.

"I didn't know she played," Holly whispers.

"Me either," I reply, even though it burns to admit it.

Within a few moments, it's clear what she's playing, and I can't keep the smile off my face.

Maren Morris's "My Church." Unlike the video I saw of Ripley belting out Carrie Underwood, this one embraces her husky voice as she adds subtle power behind it. The line about finding redemption when she gets in her car has to be a subtle jab at me for stealing the Javelin, and I laugh.

This woman. She's everything.

By the chorus, she's got everyone in the bar on their feet, singing along. There's magic in her voice, and when Holly grabs my arm and squeezes, I know she hears it too.

When Ripley whispers *thank you* into the microphone and leaves the stage, Holly is out of her seat before I am. "That's it. I want her. She's the new sound I've been dying to hear."

"Then you'll have her," Karas replies. I'm pretty sure Holly could have said she wanted the international space station, and he'd agree to get it for her. "We'll get the contracts drafted and schedule a meeting in the office. Also, the nanny just texted that Rose is fussy, so I'd like to get home."

I never thought I'd see the day that arrogant asshole Karas let his schedule be dictated by a baby, but damned if it doesn't make me like him better.

Lines of concern bracket Holly's eyes. "She is? Why didn't you say something?"

Karas looks at his wife and tucks a lock of wavy hair behind her ear. "Because this is important to you."

Tana rolls her eyes. "Damn, you two are so sweet, you're

gonna make me puke. Mick and I are staying. I'll let you know if I hear any more gems, babe."

I don't stick around to watch Holly and Tana say their good-byes because I'm already off in search of Ripley.

I catch sight of Hope behind the bar, and she must know exactly what I'm after because she points me in the direction of the employee break room.

Shoving open the door, I find Ripley putting the guitar in a case. I wait to speak until she turns around, but any words I intend to say are erased when I see the tears tracking down her face.

"Sugar, what's wrong?"

Ripley's head jerks up as though she just realized I'm standing here.

When she swipes her hands over her cheeks, trying to hide the evidence, I cross the room and pull her into my arms.

"You killed it. Why are you crying?"

With a snuffle, Ripley composes herself. "I always wanted to play onstage with my mama's guitar, but Pop smashed it when I was thirteen and finally worked up the courage to ask for lessons. He told me there was no way in hell he was going to let me parade myself on a stage like a stripper begging for dollar bills."

I could kill that old man. Straight up kill him.

"I'm so sorry. I wish I could get it back for you."

"He's going to be so pissed when he finds out I'm playing and singing, and I'm not gonna care this time. I'm done letting him control my life. He ran Mama into the ground. Chased her into another man's arms. That was on *him*. *He did that.* I'm not letting him run me down anymore. I'm done."

That's when I realize just how big of a deal it was for Ripley to take this step, and it explains why she never pursued it before. She wasn't just bogged down with work at the bar—she had an asshole of a father who shoveled years of bullshit on her.

"I'm really fucking proud of you, Ripley. You nailed it. Holly wants to sign you. She said you're the sound she's been looking for."

Ripley's eyes go wide. "What?"

"This is your shot, if you want it."

"If I want it," Ripley repeats in a whisper. "This would change everything. My whole life."

"Not everything."

"What do you mean?"

I reach out to take her hand. "What's happening between us isn't changing no matter what you decide. I don't care if you're Ripley Fischer, hot new country artist, or Ripley Fischer, bartender, as long as you're mine."

She swallows, her eyes searching my face. "Are you sure? Because right now, I have no idea what I'm going to decide."

"Am I sure that I'm crazy in love with you either way? Damn right I am."

Ripley's other hand comes up and presses to my lips. "Don't say that. You can't be. It's not—"

I kiss her fingers and move them out of the way. "I can. I am. You're the most incredible woman I've ever met, and I knew that for a fact before I ever heard you sing. It's okay if you can't say it back. I don't want to hear it until you're ready."

The door to the break room opens, and the sound of the crowd in the bar filters in.

"Rip, we need you behind the bar. Sorry, girl. Shit's

getting crazy now that the security people have left. Everyone heard that celebrities are here, and they're wanting inside."

Ripley looks over my shoulder to whoever is speaking. "I'll be right out. Just one more minute."

When the door closes again, Ripley turns back to me. "I gotta go. You should probably get out of here. They're already on the hunt for you."

"Don't worry about me. I'm not going anywhere until it's time to take you home."

"You'll be mobbed. They won't leave you alone."

I pull a shirt out of my back pocket. "Hope hooked me up."

I hold up the black T-shirt. It's an inverse of Ripley's white tank top with the White Horse Saloon logo, and when I flip it around to the back, she bursts into laughter. It reads SECURITY.

"Really?"

"Consider me your personal security tonight."

CHAPTER THIRTY-FOUR

I roll over in bed to find a note on Boone's pillow instead of the man I planned to ravage.

Where did he go? My vision still fuzzy from sleep, I blink until the blue ink comes into focus.

Sugar,
Had an early radio station interview and didn't want to
wake you. Expect a call from Homegrown Records this
morning. Holly wants to set up a meeting. I'll be home by
noon.
Love you,
Boone

Holy. Wow. A rip current of emotions threatens to drag me under as I reread the note. Being the mature adult that I am,

I pull the covers over my head and consider what in the world I'm going to do.

Holly wants to set up a meeting.

I knew it was coming, but to see it in writing is a completely different situation.

This is my shot. My chance at a life I never let myself dream about. The one my mama wanted but couldn't have because her life was cut short by someone who literally got away with murder.

Skip rip current; this is a tsunami I'm dealing with. But I can't hide under the covers all day and wait for the decision to make itself.

And then there's the rest of the note. *I'll be home . . .* Strangely enough, I feel almost as comfortable in Boone's house as I did in my old apartment above the bar. Actually, I feel more comfortable here than I do taking up space in Hope's living room on her futon. *But that doesn't mean it's my home.*

You're stalling, Rip. And yes, I am, because the last part of the note could bring me to my knees if I were standing.

Love you.

How is it possible that this incredibly generous, talented, kind man is in love with me? It feels like the cosmos is playing some kind of joke on me, but it's *real*, and that's crazy. Crazy amazing, though.

My phone vibrates from the nightstand, and I throw off the covers, shoot up in the bed, and reach for it. The number is one that I don't recognize, but I clear my throat and answer it in the most professional tone I can muster.

"Hello?"

"Hi, is this Ripley Fischer?"

"Yes, this is she."

"Wonderful! I'm Etta with Homegrown Records, and Ms. Wix would like to schedule a meeting with you at your earliest convenience. Preferably today, if possible. I know this is a little unorthodox, but she said you'd know what it pertains to. When would be the first available time in your schedule to come in? Ms. Wix is happy to accommodate you, as her schedule is still largely clear today."

"Oh. Wow. Okay. She wants me to come in today?"

"If possible. She's going to be here by eleven o'clock, unless you'd like to meet earlier."

I glance at the clock on the table. It's already eight thirty, and I need to shower, get back to Hope's to change into something resembling professional attire, and make the trip to Homegrown's office, which I'm pretty sure is right on Music Row, so not too far.

For a moment, I think about waiting for Boone and seeing if he wants to come with me, but then I straighten my shoulders. *This is about me. I can do this on my own. I'm a strong, independent woman.*

"I can be there at eleven. That would work great. Is your office on Music Row?"

Etta relays the rest of the pertinent information, and we confirm that I'll be at Homegrown Records' office to meet Holly freaking Wix at eleven o'clock.

"Thank you so much, Ms. Fischer. We'll see you this morning. I'm really looking forward to meeting you. I saw your videos, and Ms. Wix hasn't stopped talking about you."

When I hang up the phone, it feels like the grin on my face may be permanent. I run from the bed to Boone's shower and hop inside.

The whole time I'm washing up, I can't stop thinking, *Holy crap. This is really happening.*

At 10:55, I step into the outer office of Homegrown Records, and I'm suddenly worried that I'm overdressed. The weathered wooden boards of the floor look like they were salvaged from an old barn somewhere, and the giant green shag rug under the brown leather furniture resembles grass you'd see in a barnyard.

The reception desk also looks like it's made of the same reclaimed boards, and it's topped with a heavy live-edge slab of wood.

Silver letters are mounted on the wall behind the desk in a whimsical arrangement.

HOMEGROWN RECORDS

A woman with short blond hair and an angular chin pops up from behind the desk.

"Hi! You're Ripley Fischer. I recognize you from the videos. I'm Etta. We spoke this morning."

I nod. "Thank you so much for setting this up. I know I'm a few minutes early."

"Not a problem. Ms. Wix just came in with Princess Rose, so she's getting her settled in the nursery, and then she'll be ready to talk to you. We're really excited you were able to make it. Can I get you anything? Coffee? Soda? Water? Tea? Smoothie? Espresso drink? We have the most amazing coffeemaker, so if there's anything you want, I can get it for you."

Her solicitous attitude almost throws me off my game, because I'm used to being the one who's serving up drinks and making sure people are comfortable. To be on the receiving end of that treatment is completely different.

"Water would be great. Thank you."

"Of course."

She ducks down and produces a bottle of water with the Homegrown Records label on it from what must be a mini fridge beneath the desk.

"Please have a seat. Ms. Wix shouldn't be but a few minutes."

I make my way over to the seating area, and my boots sink into the plush green shag carpet. I didn't exactly know what to wear for this meeting, so I went with black slacks, a white blouse, and a black jacket that is as close to a blazer as I own. It zips up at an asymmetrical angle, and the cuffs sport thick silver buttons. My boots were the only footwear that looked remotely right with the outfit, so that's what I picked. I haven't had a lot of excess funds lately, so shoe shopping has been at the bottom of my priority list, not that it was ever near the top.

"I'm so sorry to keep you waiting." Holly's familiar voice fills the reception area as she crosses the room.

I'm glad I didn't go any fancier, because Holly's outfit is purely Nashville casual. A cream-colored sweater cinched at her waist with a thick brown belt, and skinny jeans tucked into brown heeled leather boots that come up to her knee. Gold earrings dangle to her shoulders, peeking in and out of her blond mane that looks just as good as it does on TV.

"Not at all," I say, finding my voice. "I was early. Thank you for meeting with me."

"It's my pleasure. I appreciate you coming today. I can't

tell you how happy it makes me to have you here. Come on back. We can get comfortable and talk."

I follow her through a door to the left of the reception desk, and find the inner offices of Homegrown are just as rustic as the outer.

"Creighton had the entire place redesigned and remodeled while I was out on maternity leave. I have no idea how in the hell he managed it, but he did. I wondered why he wouldn't let me come back to Nashville for weeks, but as always, that diabolical man had bigger plans. He knew once I got in this town, I'd find a way to get into my office."

The rough wood, heavy silver accents, and pops of red weren't what I'd expect with Creighton Karas heading up the project, but Holly continues.

"Would you believe he found my *Dream Office* Pinterest board that had all the pictures for inspiration? Seriously, I swear he must have worked for the CIA at some point. That board was secret, and still he managed to sniff it out and make it real, right down to the rose accents for our baby girl."

While her words would suggest she was marginally annoyed, the giant smile on her face belies them. It's clear she loves her new digs—and her husband—very much.

He's freaking terrifying, if you ask me, but then again, no one did.

We reach her corner office, where three of the four walls are solid glass. Two look out over Nashville, and the third into a nursery where a woman sits in the corner watching a tiny pink bundle sleep.

"That's Rose. Her daddy made her a princess nursery where I could watch over her while I work. The glass will frost at the touch of a button, but Crey knew I'd want to have her with me as much as possible."

"Wow. That's amazing."

"He's incredibly sweet, but don't tell him I told you. He prefers people be scared of him."

Mission accomplished, I think, but keep that to myself.

"Have a seat and we'll get down to business." She motions to a small seating area with a distressed leather love seat and two chairs.

"Thank you."

Holly grabs a file off the desk and takes the love seat, which makes me glad I picked one of the chairs.

"I know this seems kind of sudden, but that's the way this business goes. So many people become stars 'overnight' when they've actually been playing the bars and small venues for a decade. Still, when it does happen, it moves fast. So, first things first." She pins me with a direct look. "Do you want to be an overnight star? Because that's what we're fixing to do for you. Now, I have to say there are no guarantees, but in reality, with the money Homegrown is prepared to invest in you and your brand, you will be *everywhere*. Since Crey acquired the label, I haven't been focused on adding new talent, but more shoring up everything else. You're my first, and I refuse to have you be anything less than a major success. Get me?"

Even with her drawl, she's still talking fast enough that my brain is stumbling to keep up.

My brand?

Without waiting for an answer, Holly continues.

"Before you answer that question, let's talk about a couple other things, like do you write your own songs, or would you plan to only record songs written by others? We don't care either way, because honestly, a big chunk of the artists in this town don't write a word of their own music. But if you do write your own songs, I want to hear some of them, and will probably set you up with a seasoned song-writer so we can make sure they're all top-notch and sort out which ones could go on an album."

I nod and finally speak. "I do write songs. Not a lot lately, because I've been busy . . . and frankly, this has never been something I've had to think seriously about before. It's never even been in the realm of real possibilities."

Holly smiles and crosses one leg over the other. "Honey, I know. If you do this, you're still going to have trouble believing it's real six weeks or even six months from now. This is life-changing. That's why deciding whether you want to go for it is the biggest hurdle. The YouTube videos you've got out there are still getting hundreds of thousands of hits a day, especially the one of you and Frisco, so right now you're a mystery and people want to know more. If we jump on that, get you the right press and interviews, we ride the wave and keep you relevant while we prep your first album. But if you decide you don't want to do this, then it'll eventually fade after your fifteen minutes are up."

I take a deep breath and run through the thoughts that have been speeding through my mind all morning. "I don't have any other solid plans for my future right now. Literally none. I'd be an idiot not to give it a shot."

Holly leans forward on the couch. "It may seem hard to believe, but I know some of what you're feeling right now. Before I went on *Country Dreams* for my shot at a recording contract, I was deep fryin' pickles in a bowling alley in Kentucky. There's not a damn thing wrong with that because it's honest work, but I was going nowhere fast. I knew I needed one shot to get out and make something of my life, so when that chance came around, I took it. From what I understand, you've been working in a bar so long you probably don't remember what it's like to do anything else. There's also nothing wrong with that. But if you've been waiting for a chance, I'm gonna be real blunt—*this is it.*"

She pauses for a moment before continuing.

"I'm not saying Homegrown is the only label that's going to try to sign you, but I'm saying this moment, this exposure, is your shot. The other labels may not be as generous or as driven to make you a success as we are, though. I'm not trying to pressure you into choosing Homegrown, but I would be making you my personal project. And, Ripley, I don't fail when I set out to prove myself. You don't have to buy into anything I'm saying, but it's the truth. Homegrown Records will soon be a major force in this industry, and it will be my mission to take you to the top."

I wrap my arms around my middle, not sure why I feel the need to protect myself. Probably because this level of vulnerability isn't something I often show to strangers.

"It's a little scary to think of how everything would change."

"I know. I get it. But think about this." Holly studies me. "I also know what it's like to have a man at your side who is larger than life and has access to resources that seem impossible to comprehend. Crey and I will never be equals in the financial arena because he's so damned filthy rich, but I'm no slouch at earning a paycheck and standing on my own two feet. It's hard when you've got a man in your life who would happily step in and take over everything for you. But you've been doing it all on your own for so long that I can't imagine you like having to lean on Boone for help without being able to give it in return."

Damn. Score one for incredibly perceptive Holly Wix.

"How did you know?"

"Because I've got a fierce streak of pride, just like you. So what if my daddy disappeared and my mama was a deadbeat who left me on my gran's front porch and forgot to come home for years at a time? I didn't want to feel like I was worth any less than my billionaire husband, and I found my self-worth on the stages where I performed until he and I sorted our life out."

Her nonchalant recitation of her family history knocks something loose in me. That's the only explanation I have for what comes next.

"My mama was killed in the bathroom of my family's bar with the man she was cheating with. Pop was already broken, but that day he shattered. He fell into the bottom of a bottle and never found his way out. He had no problem dumping as much stuff on me as he could, but when it came down to it, there was no way I could resurrect the Fishbowl from that with no resources. I tried. I really did, but I failed."

"Oh, honey. You don't own that failure. You were set up for it, but the amazing part is that you kept that bar running for almost ten years by yourself."

My gaze cuts to her. "You know all this already?"

She nods carefully. "I told you my husband could've worked for the CIA. I probably know more about you than Boone does. But I promise, none of that information leaves this room."

With all this talk about the past, I'm feeling a little lost, and Holly must see that as well.

"If you don't want to make a decision today, you don't

have to. But in the interest of full disclosure, I'm going to tell you that the sooner you decide, the better. The hits will start to slow and interest will drop off. We want to harness the current interest and make a big splashy announcement that we've signed you, and you've got a single coming down the pipe really soon."

Movement comes from the nursery, and our attention shifts as we watch the nanny lift the pink bundle into her arms and walk with her around the room.

"If I hadn't stepped on that stage for *Country Dreams*, I wouldn't be living the life I have right now," Holly says, not looking at me but through the glass wall. "Sometimes, taking a terrifying risk leads to the most unimaginable happiness."

The reverence in her tone as she stares at her baby girl hits me deep inside.

I want this. Not Holly Wix's life, but a chance at happiness beyond what I could imagine.

I take a deep breath. "I'll do it."

CHAPTER
THIRTY-FIVE

RIPLEY

I push open the glass door of Homegrown Records with a thick silver envelope in my hand containing the contract Holly had already drawn up. I didn't sign anything yet, because even I know better than that. I need a good lawyer now, but there's no way in hell I'm calling Law.

I reach out to press the call button on the elevator, but the doors slide open before I make contact.

And out steps Amber Fleet.

Are you freaking kidding me right now?

She knocks into my shoulder as she strides past, and I'm too stunned to jump in the open elevator before the doors shut again.

I press the call button and turn to peer through the glass doors leading into Homegrown Records as I wait. Amber's high-pitched voice grows louder and louder with each word until it's impossible to miss.

"I want to see Holly Wix. She won't answer my calls or emails, but I need to talk to her."

Like the eavesdropper I apparently am, I take a step toward the glass doors so I can hear Etta's response.

"I'm sorry, Ms. Fleet. Ms. Wix's calendar is full today. I can possibly get you in next month when she's officially back full-time from maternity leave."

"Dammit, I know she's working before that." Amber rushes for the door that leads to the inner offices and grabs the handle, but it doesn't budge.

"Ms. Fleet, please understand that Ms. Wix is very busy, but I'm happy to make you an appointment for a later date."

"I need an appointment *now*."

"That's just not possible, ma'am."

"Well, you can tell Holly she's gonna regret blowing me off like this. Just wait and see." Amber spins around, and I dash back to the elevator and press the button seven times, hoping to get the hell out of here fast.

But no such luck for me today in that arena. Apparently, my luck was used up getting the career opportunity of the century.

I keep my head down, hoping Amber won't recognize me. Her heels clack against the wood, and she punches the already lit elevator button like it's somehow going to make it come faster. She releases an annoyed huff and crosses her arms, tapping her foot and mumbling something I can't make out.

She must finally look at me because the tapping stops, and I can't help but glance at her face. Her gaze is fixed on the envelope in my hands.

"She met with you, didn't she? That little bitch."

"Excuse me?" It's not until I speak that Amber's gaze lands on my face, and when it does, her features contort into an ugly mask.

"You've gotta be fucking kidding me. She met with *you*." Her words aren't so different from the thoughts I had earlier, but at least mine were missing the thick layer of malice. "She did not just sign you. No fucking way. I don't believe it."

I'm not about to give her any kind of affirmative response, so I decide to go with a benign, "Excuse me?" When the elevator doors open, I step toward them, hoping Amber is too pissed and stays behind. She doesn't.

"If this is some kind of ploy to try to keep Boone, you're going in the wrong direction. He can't handle a woman whose career is more successful than his. He'll scrape you off as soon as he finds out you were even here. I knew I was gonna get him back, but this just seals the deal."

"Excuse me?" I repeat, this time not playing dumb, but seriously confused by what she's saying.

"Do you need me to break it down into smaller words for you? You and that dumb redneck, I swear."

And I've officially heard all I need to hear. I hold up my hand.

"First, shut your face. If you want to talk shit about Boone, you're not gonna do it around me. I've thrown men three times your size out of my bar, and I guarantee I'll have no problem kicking your skinny little ass. Second, Boone didn't want you because you're a cheating whore on top of being a self-righteous bitch. So, chew on that, *Amber*. If you ever think you're getting him back, you're sadly mistaken. He's too damn smart to fall for your game again, and you'd have to do it over my dead body."

Her mouth drops open, making me wonder if this is the first time someone has given her an ass-ripping using her own brand of meanness.

"You don't know shit about shit, girl. You won't make it in this business. You're a joke."

"I'm not the one who cheated on my boyfriend and married another guy in Vegas. That was all you, Amber. By the way, thank you for fucking it up so royally that he fell in love with me."

The elevator doors open and I step out, but she's right on my heels.

"He doesn't love you! He still loves me. I know it."

"Is that why he left the engagement ring he was going to use to propose to you as a tip at the bar the night he found out what you did?"

Her eyes nearly bulge out of her head.

"What?" Her screech fills the lobby of the building.

"You lost the best thing that ever happened to you, but you better believe I'm a hell of a lot smarter. All you had to do was treat him right, and Boone would have been yours. Now he's mine, and I'm not giving him up."

I spin on my heel and make the exit of a lifetime, set to the sound of Amber Fleet's meltdown.

When I step out onto the sidewalk, the truth about what I said hits me.

I'm not giving him up . . . because I'm in love with him.

CHAPTER THIRTY-SIX

BOONE

I come home to an empty house around one o'clock. My radio interview ran over because I got sucked into telling them about the album I'm writing and how I've never had song lyrics rolling through my brain nonstop like this. There were a lot of questions about the tone of the album, but I deflected and told them they'd have to wait and see.

The note I left Ripley this morning on my pillow has been moved to the counter, and under what I wrote, she added a response.

Going to meet with Holly at 11 a.m.

My lips stretch with a smile.
That's my girl.
I'm lifting a piece of fried chicken out of the bucket when the door from the garage opens and shuts. I wait for Anthony to call out that he came inside to get some lunch, but instead Ripley blows into the house like a tornado.

"I don't care what that bitch says, you're never going to be dumb enough or desperate enough to get back together with her. *Over my dead body*." Ripley slaps a silver envelope onto the kitchen island with a decisive smack. "She can scream and cry and rant all she wants, but you see right through her now, don't you?"

Ripley's chest is heaving, and when she puts her hands on her hips, I recognize a woman on the warpath. I choose my words wisely.

"Sugar, what are you talking about?"

"Amber! She showed up at Homegrown after my appointment, screeching at the receptionist about wanting to meet with Holly, and then she turns her venom in my direction. I told her she was barking up the wrong tree if she thinks she's ever getting back with you because . . . You. Are. Mine." She punctuates each of her last three words with a slap of her hand on the island. "So I'm sorry if I overstepped, but I had to put it in terms she'd understand."

I drop the chicken into the bucket and come toward her. "Is that right?"

"Yeah, that's right. There was more, but I'm not wasting another minute thinking about that woman."

I crowd Ripley against the counter and meet her thunderous gray gaze. "I agree. I'd rather talk about your meeting with Holly."

"Before we get to that, you need to tell me what the hell you did with my car."

I lean in because her lips are dying to be kissed. I nip at the bottom one. "I stole it."

Ripley's hands flatten against my chest. "We already covered that fact."

"That's all I'm telling you for now. Drive the BMW until I tell you otherwise."

With a shove, she pushes me a step back. "You know Holly and I talked about what it's like to be with a guy who thinks he can do whatever he damn well pleases."

I use the distance she put between us to grab her hips and lift her onto the island. "Oh yeah? What else?" I tug at her lip again with my teeth, and Ripley's fingertips dig into my shoulders as she presses against me.

"You're distracting me."

"Welcome to my world, sugar. You distract me just by breathing. And now you're all riled up, the only thing I can think about is feeling that fire beneath me."

Her voice comes out in pants. "I'm strangely okay with that right about now."

"Then wrap your legs around me, because we're moving this conversation to bed."

"Do we have to?"

I meet her eyes. "The first time I fuck that tight little ass of yours isn't going to be on the kitchen counter. We can save that for the second time."

CHAPTER THIRTY-SEVEN

RIPLEY

Apparently, it's going to be a day of firsts.

My insides go liquid at Boone's words, but my legs wrap around his hips.

I've been thinking about this more than I care to admit since he initially brought it up, and today, of all days, is the one I would have picked too.

Today I conquered my fears and seized my chance at an amazing future, a future I desperately want to include this man—and not just because of how incredible he makes me feel in bed. The dirty, sexy side is a definite bonus, though.

When we get to the bedroom, Boone takes his time stripping me down to just my bra before reaching for his own shirt.

"No. Let me."

I rise off the bed and peel his T-shirt over his head before dropping to my knees in front of him to work his belt. Boone must read it in my expression, because he starts to protest when I wrap my hand around his cock.

"Sugar, I told you—"

"Stop. I want to give this to you."

Boone threads his hands into my hair. "What the hell did I do to deserve you?"

"I've been asking myself the same thing. I decided that we both got lucky."

"This isn't luck. This is hitting the jackpot of life."

I wink. "Just wait until I do this, then." I wrap my lips around his cock and suck him into my mouth.

Boone's fingers tighten on my hair, and I love the slight tug of pressure. Sucking deep, I feel tears gather at the corners of my eyes as the head of his cock hits the back of my throat. His groan fills the room.

"Goddamn, sugar."

Taking that as his stamp of approval, I keep going, feeling the answering pulse of heat between my own legs.

I want him. Want this.

And for the first time in my life, I'm going to have it all.

I continue working Boone's cock with my lips, tongue, and hands until he pulls free.

"You keep sucking me so good, I'll be coming down your throat instead of where I planned." His gaze is heavy on mine. "You trying to distract me? You change your mind?"

I shake my head. "No. I was just setting out to prove I'm no quitter."

The smile that spreads over Boone's face is *everything*.

"Sugar, I could've told you that from day one. And guess what? I'm not either. You and I are in this together. Every step of the way."

He pulls me up to my feet and takes my lips, making even more silent promises. When we break apart, Boone spins me around and presses a hand to my shoulders. I bend over the bed, my ass in the air.

"Sweet Jesus, woman. Your curves never quit." He lands a heavy hand on my right ass cheek with a smack.

Heat shimmers in the shape of a handprint on my skin. *Oh God. This is going to be intense.*

But today, right now, none of the boundaries that I'd put around my life and my dreams matter. Today, there's nothing stopping me from reaching higher and taking more. Life won't smack me down this time.

Boone drops to his knees between my legs, spreading them wider with his broad shoulders.

"What are you—"

"Hush. I'm gonna play."

And that's exactly what he does. Boone's tongue darts out as he licks me from behind, setting my nerve endings on red alert. I press up on my toes, not trying to escape but to give him more room.

"So fucking sweet. I need more."

Boone rises to his feet and flips me over on my back after unhooking my bra and leaving me completely naked. Before I can catch my breath, he's on his knees, his head between my thighs, sucking my clit between his lips and sending me over the edge.

All my inhibitions are swept away by the second orgasm that slams into me after he plunges two fingers inside, teasing my G-spot until I scream.

"Soaked, sugar. Fucking soaked."

My eyes flutter open to see Boone licking his fingers clean.

Oh. My. God. I'll never get used to that.

After he fists his cock, he thrusts inside me, fucking my pussy with long, hard strokes.

"You're too damn tempting. I had to," he says on ragged breaths.

"But—"

"Don't worry. We're getting there." Boone winks and lifts my hips higher, hitting exactly the right spot.

While I'm coming apart, he pulls free, yanks open the door to the nightstand, and pulls out the lube.

I start to roll to my stomach, but Boone stops me. "I want to see your face when we do this."

"How?" This goes to show just how much I don't know.

"Bring your knees up."

It sounds obscene, but I do it anyway. When Boone's blue eyes turn flame-hot, I know the indecent position is perfect.

No one has ever looked at me like he does. No one has ever treated me like I mattered. No one has ever put me first.

He's it. He's the one.

The knowledge sweeps through me, coinciding with Boone's thumb lubing me up and coating his cock before he fits the head against the hole that was previously a no-go zone.

"You ready, sugar? We'll take it slow. You want to stop, you say the word, and we stop."

"I'm done stopping. I'm done taking it slow. I want this, Boone. I want you."

He leans down to take my mouth in a deep kiss at the same time he presses inside me. I suck in a breath as he keeps his forehead resting against mine.

"Oh my God. Oh my God. Oh my God."

"You okay?"

I nod, even though *okay* isn't the word for what I'm feeling. Exhilarated and one step from losing my ever-loving mind would be more accurate.

Holy hell, why did I put this off so long?

Boone continues forward until his balls touch my ass. "Sweet fucking Christ. This may not last long. You're so goddamned tight." Strain marks his forehead, and sweat beads on mine. "Gotta move now, sugar."

"Do it. Please."

Boone reaches between us to press his thumb against my clit as he pulls out and then surges back in. My scream takes us both by surprise, and so does my almost-instant orgasm.

"Boone!" His name echoes off the ceiling, and I don't care who hears it. I lose myself to the sensation as he continues to thrust while teasing my clit.

Oh. My. God.

Within minutes, I'm limp, and Boone empties himself inside me with a hoarse shout of my name. My eyelids flutter closed and I'm boneless, floating on a cloud of pleasure I never knew possible. When he finally pulls free of my body and returns with a damp towel to clean us up, I'm still without words.

"Come on. Let's get you in the shower."

Boone lifts me into his arms and carries me into the bathroom, not setting me on my feet until we're in the glass enclosure with the water beating down.

My limbs are unsteady but I have Boone to lean on, and I finally let myself do exactly that.

CHAPTER THIRTY-EIGHT

BOONE

With Ripley in one of my T-shirts and a pair of boxer shorts, we make our way back to the kitchen.

"I'm starving," she says over the rumble of her stomach.

"Then let's get you fed."

I snag the bucket of chicken from where I left it and offer it to her.

"Oh, hell yes." She tears into a piece and shoves the silver envelope on the counter toward me with her free hand. "I said yes. Well, technically I said I'd say yes after a lawyer gives me the all-clear."

Only Ripley would be so casual about signing a record deal.

"This calls for champagne, sugar." I spin around and yank open the fridge to grab my just-in-case bottle of Dom from beside the ketchup. When I pull it out, Ripley laughs.

"It's such a cliché that you keep bottles of Dom handy in your fridge."

"You never know when you're going to need to celebrate. Plus, Ma loves this stuff, and I keep it on hand for her when she comes."

Ripley shakes her head at me but watches as I produce two glasses, pop the cork, and pour. "It's like you've done this before."

"A time or two. Life's too short not to celebrate every chance you get. And today, this is all about you. I'm really fucking proud of you, sugar. I think you're making the right move. Cheers to you and an amazing future."

She accepts a glass of champagne and lifts it to clink against mine. "Cheers to us. Because I wouldn't be in this position if not for you." She pauses. "But I don't want you to ever think that me falling in love with you has a damn thing to do with this. Because it doesn't."

I freeze with my glass to my lips. "What did you say?"

Her face goes soft, losing that guarded edge she's always had. "I'm falling in love with you, but it doesn't have anything to do with—"

I come around the island and lower my glass to the granite.

"Stop right there so we can get a couple things straight. First, you're not falling in love with me, Ripley. You're already there. You've been there since you charged a bull to get to me. Maybe before, but that's when I knew it for sure. I will *never* think this has anything to do with it, because you've made it clear in every word and action that you don't expect a damn thing from me. But you know what? That just makes me want to give you even more. Because you won't ask for it. You don't expect it." I pause and meet those stormy gray eyes. "Ripley, if you'll let me, I'll give you everything."

A small smile turns up the corners of her trembling lips. "How about we start with you giving me my car back?"

CHAPTER
THIRTY-NINE

RIPLEY

I fell asleep with Boone wrapped around me and woke up the same way. In the early-morning hours, he made love to me in his bed, telling me how beautiful I was and how glad he was to have me in his life.

Before we drifted off again, he whispered, "Never letting you go."

I feel the exact same way.

When I wake up the second time, it's to an empty bed. I pop out of it when I hear a door close somewhere else in the house. I toss Boone's T-shirt on and make a mental note to bring some clothes over later so I'm not constantly stealing his.

I peek my head out of the bedroom, and my jaw drops.

It appears Boone beat me to it. He walks toward me loaded down with two duffel bags that I recognize and a box.

"I went to Hope's and got your stuff. I was gonna ask if you wanted to officially move in, but I decided to skip that step."

"Are you sure?"

"Absofuckinglutely. I want to be able to wake up with you every damned day."

Maybe it was the early-morning orgasm, or maybe the fact that the glow of my declaration of love is still so fresh, but I decide not to argue.

"Okay."

This time it's Boone wearing the look of surprise. "Okay?"

"Yeah. I'm good with it. I mean, Esteban is already here . . ."

"I knew keeping the parrot was a smart move." Boone winks at me and carries my stuff into the bedroom.

Two hours later, I finally pull on my own clothes, and Boone and I head out to meet with one of his lawyers to go over the contract. Holly already sent it to them via email, and now he wants to go over the details in person.

"Don't you have something else you should be doing?" I ask Boone as traffic slows near downtown.

"Something more important than making sure you know exactly what you're signing up for with this? Definitely not."

"But I thought you were supposed to be writing a new album and—"

"I did."

My head jerks to the side. "What?"

Boone's smile could light up the cab of the truck. "Turns out you're a hell of a muse. I've written forty-seven songs since the day we met, and fourteen of them are going on my next album."

"Are you serious? Holy shit."

"I know I make it look easy, but I worked my ass off when you weren't around so I could take every chance I had to spend time with you."

A warmth spreads through me, and I reach out to squeeze Boone's hand. He doesn't let go, but instead keeps our fingers interlocked all the way to the parking garage.

Two hours later, my signature is on the bottom of a contract with Homegrown Records. Boone's lawyer—actually, now *my* lawyer—negotiated the points he had issues with over the phone with Homegrown's counsel, and we made a deal.

Once my signed copy is emailed to Holly, I get a call. I put it on speaker because it's only Boone and me in the small conference room now.

"Hell yes, girl! This is going to be freaking phenomenal! Get ready, because we're prepping the press release, and you're going to be on everyone's radar in a few hours."

Boone wraps his arm around me and pulls me into his lap.

"Thank you so much for the opportunity, Holly. I'm incredibly excited."

"You and me both. Gotta go. I'll be in touch."

Boone presses a kiss to my forehead. "I think it's time for another bottle of Dom and a hell of a fancy dinner."

CHAPTER FORTY

I t doesn't take long for the news to spread like wildfire. Boone and I left a restaurant a few hours later, and the cameras were flashing along with the questions being tossed at us. Instead of answering, I waved and climbed into the back of the SUV Anthony drove us in, expecting this kind of reaction.

My phone immediately started going nuts too. It seemed that every single person I've ever known has something to say to me now that I'm *somebody*. After I told Hope the ink was dry on the contract, I didn't answer any calls. Hope was thrilled for me, but sad that I was leaving the White Horse, although she did extend an invitation for me to come back and perform anytime I want.

Even her making the offer was surreal.

I turn my phone off for the rest of the night, and when I turn it on in the morning, I immediately wish I hadn't. Seventeen new voice mails.

File those under *nope, not happening*.

Boone and I are making breakfast in the kitchen after an

amazing morning of shutting out the world when Anthony pokes his head inside the house.

"Boss, I got a guy out at the gate who's looking to talk to Ms. Fischer."

I close the fridge after retrieving a carton of orange juice. "A reporter?" I ask, which is just another indication of how much my life has changed overnight. Holly was absolutely right about that.

Anthony shakes his head and holds out a card. "Says he's a private investigator."

That's when I remember the mortgage Pop took out on the Fishbowl to hire a PI.

Boone grabs the card and brings it over to me.

MORTON TWINING
PRIVATE INVESTIGATOR

I look to Boone. "He has to be the one investigating Mama's murder."

"You want to talk to him?"

Both men are watching me as I weigh the question. Finally, I reply.

"I want to put the past behind me so I can move on. Let it go. If he's figured something out, then I want to know."

"It's totally up to you, sugar."

I give Anthony a nod. "Let him in."

"Will do, boss lady."

Anthony shuts the door behind him, and Boone glances down at my bare legs.

"You might want to find some pants first."

Morton Twining is quite possibly the most unassuming man I've ever met. He can't be more than an inch taller than me, and although his frame isn't frail, it's definitely not bulky. His light brown hair is thin on top, and his khaki-colored jacket conceals a red-and-blue plaid shirt tucked into khaki pants.

He's very . . . blah.

Once we're seated in the living room, introductions out of the way, Mr. Twining asks his first question.

"Did you publish any songs under your name about twenty years ago, Ms. Fischer?"

What the hell?

"Excuse me?" Boone stiffens on the couch beside me.

Mr. Twining pulls a folder from his brown leather brief-case and lays it on the coffee table. "Since I took on this case, I've been doing a lot of digging in odd places, and one of those places led me to four songs published by Ripley Fischer and Gil Green twenty years ago."

The name Gil Green stands out like a beacon. "Gil Green was my mother's . . . They were . . ."

Twining nods. "Yes, I'm aware. Which is why I thought it was odd that your name was attached to them. The royalties have been accruing to a trust in Green's estate all this time, and no one thought anything of it until his wife passed away about three weeks ago. The lawyers couldn't figure out who Ripley Fischer was and why she was the beneficiary of this particular trust."

Boone squeezes my hip. "That's really friggin' weird."

"Indeed, which is why I wanted to confirm with you that these weren't part of some pet project you and Green might have done when you were a child."

I shake my head. "No. I only met him in passing a couple

times. He gave me a guitar once. We never had any kind of relationship."

Twining shuts his briefcase and rises from his seat.

"That's it?"

"I suspect I'll have more questions for you, and the estate will be in touch. Soon, I'd bet. I'm getting closer, but the trail is taking an unexpected turn."

"Unexpected how?"

He dodges the question. "I'll be in touch, Ms. Fischer. You can keep those copies. I thought you might like to see some of what I assume is your mother's work."

And with that, Boone leads him out of the living room.

Well, isn't that just the weirdest freaking thing? I pick up the folder off the table and flip it open to the first page of sheet music. It's a duet about forbidden love.

Nope. Not reading it. It's not like I need more proof of my mother's infidelity.

The name of the second song gives me pause.

"Envy Green on the Vine."

The lyrics are terrible, but I read them anyway. It's all about wanting what someone else has, and wondering how far they'll go to take it from you.

Shivers prickle into chill bumps on my skin.

Who were they writing about? My mom being envious of Gil Green's wife? Or someone being envious of what my mom had?

I get to the final verse and read it three times.

From the stage in that bar,
  I play my guitar,
  waiting for a knife in my back.
  But as we pile on those lies,

I thank God that I
hid the truth behind
old Willie's eyes.

It feels like it should mean something, but it makes absolutely no freaking sense.

Who would Mama have been waiting for a knife in the back from? Or was it Gil who feared someone? And what the hell does it mean to hide the truth behind old Willie's eyes?

Boone comes back into the living room. "You okay?"

I nod and look back at the lyrics again before handing the page to him. "Will you read this? That last verse is totally throwing me off."

He takes the paper and his eyes move back and forth as he reads the words. "How can you hide the truth behind someone else's eyes? That part doesn't make sense to me either."

"I have no idea. It doesn't—" I cut myself off. "Wait. Willie. Willie Nelson. There's a picture of him in the bar. What if . . . what if this really is about my mama, and she hid something behind it?" I know I sound crazy, but my suggestion isn't that much crazier than these lyrics.

"Behind the picture? Really? You think she would have?"

"I don't know, but if she were going to hide something, that wouldn't be a bad place. It's not like anyone would look. Those things are screwed to the wall. No one ever moves them, and nothing has been added since Mama died. She was the one who put them all in frames and hung them herself."

Boone sits down on the couch next to me. "You really want to dig into this?"

Part of me wants to say no, because I've just accepted an opportunity that's going to completely change my future. But a bigger part says now is the time to put the past to rest so I can let it go.

"This has been hanging over my head for two-thirds of my life. It's always been the unanswered question, and I feel like I need closure. Maybe then I could move on and focus on the future."

Boone nods. "All right. So, what do you want to do?"

"I think I need to go to the Fishbowl."

CHAPTER
FORTY-ONE

BOONE

Going back to the Fishbowl wasn't on my list of things to do today, but there's no way I'm letting Ripley go by herself. Last we heard, Ripley's dad hasn't been arrested or charged based on the video evidence that had gotten the charges against me dropped. I suspect it's because the cops want to put the case behind them rather than getting involved in proceedings that will constantly highlight the fact that they screwed up.

Even so, Brandy knows Ripley turned the tape in, and I'm not taking a chance of Brandy getting a shot at her. On top of that, I don't care if we're talking about a twenty-year-old cold case, the murderer is still out there.

"Can you pull up the security feeds on my laptop? See if there's anyone there?"

Ripley's eyebrows shoot up. "That's a good idea."

"Have a few of those now and again."

She rises on her toes to press a kiss to my lips. "How about you have an awesome idea later when we're naked?"

"Deal."

She flips open the laptop and pulls up the website. Except instead of seeing the inside of the bar like I did the last time she pulled up this page, it's just black. Ripley hits a couple of keys and nothing happens.

"Dammit. They must have disabled the cameras after the cops confronted Brandy with the video."

Shit. "So that means we're going in blind."

Ripley nods, but there's a new apprehension in the set of her shoulders. "If we can get in at all. What if they changed the locks?"

"I guess we're about to find out."

We load up in the truck and head downtown.

The Fishbowl looks completely empty from the outside. No cars out front, and no one parked in the back.

When Ripley reaches for her door handle of the truck, I put a hand on her thigh. "If your cousin is inside, I doubt she's going to be happy to see us."

With a grimace, she replies. "True. If she's inside, then we bail, and I move on and leave this for the PI to handle."

"You sure?"

She bites her lip. "I really want her not to be there."

"Then let's go." I hold out my hand. "Keys?"

She drops the keys in my palm.

"All right. If we do run into her, you're telling her you left something behind and had to come back and get it. She doesn't need to know anything else."

"I agree. I could be coming back for that ring. The one you left in the bar. That you got for Amber. It's still here. I hid it so Brandy wouldn't find it and hock it. I wanted to get it anyway. There's no point in leaving it here."

That engagement ring is basically the last thing I ever want back, but if we need an excuse, it'll work.

"Fine, but we're unloading it immediately. I don't want it around."

"That's fair. We could sell it and donate the proceeds to charity."

"Deal. Now, let's get in there and get out."

I climb out of the truck, shut the door, and walk around the front. Ripley's beside me when I shove the key in the lock and turn.

Click. It opens.

"Oh good," Ripley whispers as she follows me inside the bar. It's dark and quiet, much like it was the day of the bird-napping. Ripley pulls a penlight from her pocket and flips it on.

"Really?"

She shrugs. "Seemed like a good idea so we don't have to turn on all the lights." She heads directly for the center of the wall across from the bar, zeroing in on the photograph of Willie Nelson. "Damn. I didn't bring a screwdriver. There's a toolbox in the office." She steps away from the picture, but I pull out my pocketknife.

"I got this." I move to the frame and use the tip of the blade to remove the screws holding it onto the wall. Together, we lift off the dust-covered picture of Willie.

Ripley flips it over, and at first, I see nothing but the back of a yellowed sheet that looks like it came in the frame. But when Ripley peels it away, another piece of paper falls free.

"What is that?" I squint at it as she focuses the flashlight on the faded handwriting.

"I don't know." She scans the paper and locks onto the signature at the bottom. "Holy shit. It's a letter from my mama."

She begins to read it out loud.

If you're finding this, I'm guessing I'm not around anymore. There have been plenty of days I've thought about what it would be like to do the deed myself, but I couldn't leave my little girl alone in this world.

Ripley blinks, tears shimmering in her eyes. "Oh my God."

She deserves better than this life, and I'm trying to give it to her. I know everyone's thinking the worst, but sometimes you have to let them smear you if there's a bigger purpose down the road. I've never cheated on my husband. Not with anyone, including Gil. Despite what everyone's saying, I'm not pining away, hoping he'll leave his wife. I don't feel that way about him. He's just a nice customer who saw me with bruises one too many times and finally forced me to tell him what was going on.

It takes a lot out of a woman's pride to admit she hasn't walked out on the man who hits her. Gil wanted to help me make a future outside this bar, and I've been hoping that's what my songs will do. I figured if anything happened to me, at least the money would end up going to my baby girl.

Whoever's reading this letter, can you make sure she knows I did it for her? Who knows, maybe one of them will end up a number-one hit, and she'll never have to worry about money for the rest of her life. All she has to do is talk to Gil, and he'll make sure she gets what's coming to her. He set up a fancy trust so Frank can never get his hands on a dime of it.

He's gotten enough from me.

Blood.

Sweat.

Tears.

I'm done with it.

My bag is packed, and tomorrow I'm finally doing it. I'm leaving my husband, and I'm taking my baby girl with me. I don't know what's going to happen, but the feeling in my gut tells me that having a backup plan might be smart.

I just hope I don't lose my nerve.

Either way, I'd be really grateful if you'd make sure this letter gets to Ripley Fischer. She always deserved better than everyone calling her mama a whore, but at least this way she'll know it wasn't true. I'm not the type to be unfaithful. I'm better than that.

All I want is for my baby to have a life where she can hold her head high and be proud of where she came from.

If something happens to me, all you need to do is look close to home. Frank is on a hair trigger, and I've always wondered if he'd just push me down the stairs one day and be done with it. But I'm too useful to put out of commission permanently, I suspect. Then there's Laurelyn waiting in the wings to step into my place. She always wanted what I have, so my leaving should make her really happy. She's welcome to Frank, since she always said he should've been hers to begin with anyway.

I'm done.

—Rhonda Fischer

P.S. Tell my girl I love her. She's the best thing that ever happened to me.

Tears are running down Ripley's face when she meets my gaze in the darkness of the bar.

"She . . . she wasn't . . ." Her words are interrupted by a hiccup. "How could I not have known? All this time? I thought—"

The lights to the bar flip on, momentarily blinding us both.

"You thought exactly what we all thought."

CHAPTER
FORTY-TWO

RIPLEY

Aunt Laurelyn comes toward Boone and me, a gun in her hand.

"And what everyone else is going to keep on thinkin'. So just drop that right on the floor and back up. Then you're gonna tell me where that diamond ring is Brandy said you stashed here."

My brain is working overtime, trying to put the pieces together.

Mama thought Laurelyn wanted Pop. Pop was out in the bar when she was killed . . . and as far as I know, the cops never questioned my aunt about the murder.

"Why?" I breathe the word.

Laurelyn waves the gun. "I didn't open it up to question-and-answer time. Now, give me whatever it is you've got there, and tell me where the damned ring is."

All the saliva in my mouth dries up as I focus on the barrel of the old pistol, and memories come crashing together in my brain. It's the gun Pop always kept behind the bar. He used to let me watch him clean it sometimes.

It went missing when Mama was murdered and was never found. The cops presumed it was the murder weapon, which is why they took Pop in for questioning, even though he was making drinks when the murder happened.

"Where did you get the gun, Laurelyn?"

My aunt centers it on me. "Been carrying it around a long, long time."

I don't even have to ask her if she did it. I know she did. And then she hugged me afterward and bought me a goddamned Happy Meal.

"Why? She was leaving anyway. If you wanted Pop, she was going to let you have him."

Boone stills beside me, and I can almost hear him cursing me in his brain.

"I didn't know that! I didn't know until we found a damned packed bag upstairs and it was already done!"

"But how? I was the first one inside, and there was no one else in the bathroom."

None of it makes any sense. When I skidded to a halt on the tile, there was only Mama and Gil, dead on the floor.

Laurelyn shakes her head at me and laughs. "Says who? I jumped on the toilet in the stall and closed the door. When you ran out—"

"You snuck out and pretended to break down when you saw them."

She shakes her head. "Something like that. It wasn't like I planned it. Frank was drinking as much as he was serving, so I took the gun from behind the bar and tucked it in my pants because I didn't trust him not to shoot up the place. Maybe I should've let him. And then I walked into the bathroom and saw them in there together . . . and I just . . . I couldn't stand to see her humiliate her Frank one more time under his own goddamned roof. He deserved better than that! He stayed by her, even with the rumors going around."

The confession crashes into me, and I'm horrified to finally hear the truth. Before I can think of a single thing to say, Laurelyn waves the gun around.

"Tell me where you hid that damned ring. Brandy said that rock is worth at least ten Gs, and I need the money more than either of you."

Boone finally speaks. "Ma'am, I'll give you all the money you want and you can get the hell out of here. All you have to do is put the fucking gun down."

"Shut your mouth, boy. I didn't ask you."

"Mama? Are you down here?"

Brandy's voice comes from upstairs before I hear the creak of footsteps on the old treads.

Oh shit. I don't know how Aunt Laurelyn's going to cover up this one, but I know there's no way in hell she'll shoot her own daughter. I look to Boone, but his eyes are fixed on the gun that wobbles in Laurelyn's hand as she glances toward the stairs.

"Hold on, girl. I'm coming back up."

The treads keep creaking.

"I told you to wait upstairs," Laurelyn yells at Brandy when she hits the bottom step.

My aunt's arm bobs as she looks away, and Boone launches himself at her, tackling her to the floor like he did with the rodeo clown. A shot explodes from the gun, deafeningly loud. Both Laurelyn and Boone go still, and Brandy shrieks.

"No!" I scream and bolt toward them.

I can't handle a replay of what happened at the rodeo, and I'm not losing another person I love in this goddamned bar.

Before I can drop to my knees, Boone rolls off my aunt, keeping both her hands pinned over her head. Thankfully, I don't see blood coming from him.

"Oh my God, are you okay?"

"Yeah," he grunts before he knocks Laurelyn's hands against the floor, and she finally releases her grip on the gun.

"Help!"

Brandy's wail finally gets through to me, and I see her on the floor at the base of the stairs, dark red staining her pink shirt. *But how?*

I rush to her side. "Where are you hit?"

"I don't know. What's going on? Who has a gun?"

"Call 911," Boone orders from where he has my aunt pinned to the floor. He looks to Brandy and then back to me. "Must have been a ricochet or something."

"Brandy!" Aunt Laurelyn yells, and Brandy's gaze cuts to her mom.

"Mama? You shot me?"

"I told you to stay upstairs," Laurelyn spits out.

Like I did with Boone at the rodeo, I sacrifice my shirt and use it to put pressure on Brandy's wound. "Hold this on there. Tight. I'm calling for an ambulance."

Once I get a dispatcher on the line and fill her in on the situation, Brandy lifts the shirt off the wound. At the sight of her own blood, her eyes roll back in her head and she slumps to the floor, unconscious.

When I relay that to the dispatcher, the woman promises help is on the way.

The cops get there first, then the PI with Pop in tow. Apparently, they figured out the clues in the lyrics and were coming to investigate the bar too, but they didn't expect to walk into pandemonium.

"Jesus fucking Christ. Is someone gonna tell me what the hell happened here?"

CHAPTER FORTY-THREE

BOONE

Hours later, after being interviewed by multiple cops, telling our stories over and over, and listening to Ripley's father being questioned, Ripley and I are finally allowed to go home. She's been holding it together like a champ, but I know the break is coming. I can feel it.

It happens as we pull into the garage at my house.

"Her own sister?"

I hop out of the truck and open Ripley's door to lift her into my arms and carry her inside.

Ripley's father confirmed to the police that twenty years ago, his sister-in-law had indeed told him that his wife was having affairs. Since the man apparently doesn't know how to handle anything head-on, his solution was to drown himself in the bottle and take out his anger on his wife and daughter. He never even confronted Rhonda to find out if it was true. After Rhonda and Gil Green were murdered, Laurelyn had offered him more than a shoulder to cry on for comfort.

Frank had been adamant when he said there was no way he would have touched his sister-in-law. He wouldn't even look at her, because she looked too much like his dead wife and he didn't want any reminders.

He never realized that by telling Laurelyn to pack her shit up and leave, he was giving her the perfect out to escape the consequences of her actions.

Brandy wasn't shot. The bullet had gone wild and shattered a picture across the room, sending a piece of glass flying that sliced into her like shrapnel. Physically, she was fine after being patched up with a butterfly bandage, but watching her mother being led away in handcuffs had left her unhinged. I can still hear her screaming at her mama that she always knew she didn't love her enough.

Laurelyn hit back, telling Brandy she would never have come back to Nashville if it weren't for the bar and Frank. We could hear Brandy's hysterical screeching even as we left the building.

Now, Ripley's tears soak my shoulder as she sobs. I sit down on the couch in the living room where the sheet music still lies on the table, and hold her on my lap.

She snuffles and hiccups before lifting her head. "I've thought the worst of her all these years. I never once thought there was a chance that she didn't cheat. What kind of daughter am I?"

"Sugar, you can't blame yourself for that. You thought exactly what you were told to think as a kid. Why would you have questioned it? The evidence was all right there, supporting everything you were told."

"But they were wrong and . . . God, I feel like I don't even know who I am right now."

"I'll tell you who you are—the strongest, most incredible woman I've ever met."

She rocks against me. "That's not true. I never once thought . . . And the truth was *right there*."

"And you saw it. You found it. You put the pieces together, and now you can tell the world what really happened, if you want."

"If Laurelyn had just stayed away . . ."

I glance at the sheet music on the table. "I suspect the private investigator probably shook her loose and had her starting to worry, plus she said she couldn't pass up the chance to make some easy money at the bar. Coming back to the scene of the crime let her keep an eye on things, just in case the PI was getting too close."

Ripley nods. "What happens now?"

"They charge her, and hopefully she pleads guilty."

"If she doesn't, then we've got a whole public circus of a trial."

My shoulders tense at the thought. That's the last thing she needs right now, and I hope like hell the confession from Laurelyn and our statements will be enough.

"No matter what happens, we'll face it together. You and me, sugar. A package deal, and one hell of a team."

Ripley meets my gaze, her stormy eyes even cloudier than normal with the sheen of tears. "Why would you throw yourself at her? She could've killed you!" Her panic is delayed, but not surprising.

"You think I wouldn't take a bullet for you? You charged a pissed-off bull for me."

"I didn't think—"

"Well, I did, and there was no way in hell I was going to

live the rest of this life without you. If letting her shoot me would keep you breathing, then so be it."

"You really do love me," Ripley says, her tone hushed.

"You're just figuring this out?"

She shakes her head and wraps her arms around my neck. "No, but don't you dare ever do anything like that again. I need you breathing to be happy. So, let's work on both of us staying alive."

"Deal," I tell her as I press a kiss to her lips and lift her into my arms.

Esteban cocks his head at us and fluffs his wings. *"Lovebirds."*

The damned parrot always gets it right.

CHAPTER FORTY-FOUR

Twenty years later, the questions surrounding the murder of country legend Gil Green have finally been put to rest, and it's not what the guidebooks told you. Rhonda Fischer, late wife of Frank Fischer, proprietor of the infamous Fishbowl bar, finally got her say. A letter from the slain woman was entered into evidence at the trial of her sister, Laurelyn Lear, who agreed to a plea bargain. Sentencing is scheduled for later this week.

Fischer's daughter, Ripley, now finds herself in the spotlight for a completely different reason. She and country music darling Holly Wix have released a brand-new duet. "Don't Tell Me No" debuted at #1 on the country charts and is the first single off Ripley Fischer's freshman album, *Finding Myself*, which is slated to release next month.

Fischer has also been making headlines as the woman at country music bad boy Boone Thrasher's side. The couple recently made a hefty joint donation at a Nashville pet shelter where the couple adopted a dog. Thrasher announced yesterday that he and Fischer will be touring together next year.

Thrasher's latest album hits stores in two weeks, and is rumored to include several songs written for Fischer. The release of the latest single gives credence to that, as fans were stunned when they learned the chart-topping hit was actually a marriage proposal.

Fischer publicly stated that since Thrasher put the question in a song, he'll have to wait for her answer in one too.

EPILOGUE

RIPLEY

Three months later

My gaze darts from one person to the next while Boone tries to explain the Karas family tree to me, but I'm lost. I don't think it's crazy, because I dare anyone to try to figure this out during the course of one baptism.

How many secrets can one family have?

Apparently, when it comes to the Karas family, a lot.

Creighton's sister, Greer, and her husband, Cavanaugh Westman, a guy I've only previously seen in movies, accept the solemn duty of being godparents to the squirming baby in white lace.

Rose and I are quite well acquainted now that I spend a good deal of time at Homegrown Records. After all, once a baby spits up on you, there's a sort of bond that's formed—less official, but still sacred.

It's not until after Rose is placed back in Holly's arms

and the remainder of the standing, sitting, and kneeling happens that the service is over and we follow the crowd to a massive fancy white tent set up behind the church. At least a dozen men wearing dark suits are set up as security, and one checks identification for a second time before letting us in.

"They have more security here than they did last week," I whisper to Boone.

Last week we attended an event that was so incredibly surreal, I still can't believe it actually happened. I walked down a red carpet, and while I've done that before, it never gets old, and then I *performed at a freaking awards show*.

I was so insanely terrified, but the woman proudly watching as her baby is passed around today calmed my nerves by giving me a slightly creepy alternative to *picture them in their underwear*.

"Just pretend that if anyone says or does anything mean, Crey will make sure they disappear."

Staring at all the security, especially the guys flanking an older man who looks like he stepped straight out of *The Godfather*, I'm starting to wonder if Holly wasn't joking.

Before I can quietly ask Boone if bullets are going to start flying, the older man walks up to Creighton, who has reclaimed baby Rose, with open arms.

"The first of a new generation. She's a perfect little princess."

Holly steps forward. "Dom, don't you even start. Crey already spoils her something fierce."

"She's my granddaughter, and I'll spoil her however I want," Dom replies as he leans forward to press a kiss to each of Holly's cheeks. "She is perfection. You have done us proud, my dear."

A heavily tattooed man—at least I assume he's heavily tattooed, because even his thick beard and man bun can't hide the ink curling up out of the collar of his shirt—wraps his arm protectively around the woman to the left of me.

"You just wait. When he finds out I knocked you up, he's gonna send his goons down for a shotgun wedding."

"Shhh. I'll tell him when we're ready. Not a minute before." The woman covers the tattooed hand on her belly with her own as she looks around. She catches my gaze on her and raises an eyebrow. "You're sworn to secrecy. I may not look tough, but I was a mob princess before mob princesses were cool." She blinks. "Wait, maybe they've never been cool. Okay, yeah, scratch that. We're still not cool. At least, I'm not."

The tatted-up guy's body is visibly shaking with laughter. "Calm down, cupcake. I'm sure they're not going to narc on you." He turns and holds out his hand to me. "I'm Bishop. This is Eden. I can also attest to the fact that she's pretty damn cool."

Boone and I both shake his hand. "I recognize you. You had a spread in *Inked Life* this month."

Eden claps her hands. "That's definitely him. See, babe, you're famous now." She glances at Boone's tattoos, also not completely covered by his suit. "You should come down to NOLA. Voodoo Ink is the *best* tattoo shop around."

Boone looks over at me. "Maybe if I can talk her into marrying me, we'll head down there as a honeymoon. I've always loved New Orleans."

I elbow Boone in the ribs, but softly. Kinda. "Would you stop saying that to people?"

"What? That I've been carrying around a ring for three weeks, but you still won't give me an answer?"

I roll my eyes. "Don't listen to him. He isn't carrying a ring. He just likes to joke—"

"Oh, sugar, someday you're gonna realize I don't joke around with shit when it comes to you."

I shoot him a shocked look, but secretly I'm thrilled because I've got a newly recorded song on my phone, finally perfected and ready for Boone to hear.

Eden looks from me back to Boone. "Looks like you're going to have some interesting conversations after this."

Boone pulls me into his side. "Every conversation with this woman is interesting."

Before I can reply, a ruckus of some sort breaks out at the entrance to the tent, and two security guys have a third man by the arms.

"Get your fucking hands off me." The restrained man is the epitome of tall, dark, and scarily handsome.

Creighton hands Rose to Holly and strides toward him.

"What the hell are you doing here, Cannon? You weren't invited."

A hush sweeps over the crowd in the tent, and the two men eye each other like they should be holding pistols at twenty paces, or however many paces dueling pistols require.

"We need to talk, Crey."

"And you decide my daughter's baptism is the right place? Get the hell out."

The older man, Dom, watches the scene with interest.

"Just hear me out."

"I don't have to do a damn thing."

"Five minutes," Cannon says from between clenched teeth, and I get the feeling this is taking a toll on his pride.

Holly steps up to Creighton's side. "Talk to him. But do it somewhere else so our guests can enjoy the afternoon and not watch the two of you beat the hell out of each other."

Creighton's stiff posture doesn't relax, but he strides out of the tent with a clipped "Follow me" tossed over his shoulder.

Once they're gone and the crowd in the tent resumes chatting quietly, Holly, Greer, and Cav join Boone and me where we stand with Eden and Bishop.

"Anyone else want to lay odds on how that turns out?" Greer asks.

Cav looks down at her. "Really, babe?"

"What? It's not like they're going to kill each other. They went into a church. I'm pretty sure even God wouldn't hesitate to strike Crey down for that."

"Oh, shush. Crey knows that it wouldn't be God he'd have to worry about. I'd kill him myself if he did that on Rose's baptism day," Holly says with a smile in her voice.

These people are all nuts. That's my official opinion.

By the time we walk toward my gorgeous and completely restored Javelin an hour later, Creighton has returned and the other man disappeared.

"Do you think . . ."

Boone snags the keys from my palm. "I don't want to know."

I lunge for the keys. "Hey, my car, I drive."

"Not this time, sugar. I'm driving, and we're not going home until I get the answer I want."

I smile, smug with the knowledge of my secret. "Fine, but I'm picking the music."

The End

Cannon's story is next in the Dirty world!

Visit www.meghanmarch.com/subscribe to sign up for my newsletter, and be the first to know when it's coming. Also, you'll never miss another announcement about upcoming projects, new releases, sales, exclusive excerpts, and give-aways. Haven't read Holly and Creighton's story yet? You can start the Dirty Billionaire Trilogy for free! Greer and Cav's story is found in the Dirty Girl Duet, and you can get all the dirt on Bishop and Eden in *Beneath These Shadows*, a standalone in the Beneath series.

ACKNOWLEDGEMENTS

I'm starting to lose count of how many books I've written, but one thing I can never lose sight of is how blessed I am to have amazing readers. Thank you for following me on this journey. I can't wait to give you more stories.

To my entire team, I love you all, and I couldn't do this without you. Let's keep doing this for a long, long time, okay?

ALSO BY MEGHAN MARCH

Defiant Queen

Sinful Empire

ABOUT THE AUTHOR

Making the jump from corporate lawyer to romance author was a leap of faith that *New York Times*, #1 *Wall Street Journal*, and *USA Today* bestselling author Meghan March will never regret. With over thirty titles published, she has sold millions of books in nearly a dozen languages to fellow romance-lovers around the world. A nomad at heart, she can currently be found in the woods of the Pacific Northwest, living her happily ever after with her real-life alpha hero.

She would love to hear from you.
Connect with her at:
www.meghanmarch.com

Made in the USA
Middletown, DE
03 May 2024